W9-AAI-387

MOUNTAINS STAND STRONG

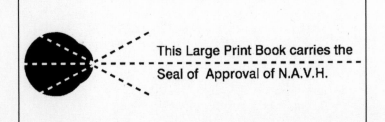

This Large Print Book carries the
Seal of Approval of N.A.V.H.

MOUNTAINEER DREAMS, BOOK ONE

MOUNTAINS STAND STRONG

IRENE B. BRAND

THORNDIKE PRESS
A part of Gale, Cengage Learning

GALE
CENGAGE Learning

Detroit • New York • San Francisco • New Haven, Conn • Waterville, Maine • London

GALE
CENGAGE Learning™

LIBRARY OF CONGRESS CATALOGING-IN-PUBLICATION DATA

Brand, Irene B., 1929–
  Mountains stand strong / by Irene B. Brand.
    p. cm. — (Mountaineer dreams series ; #1) (Thorndike Press large print Christian historical fiction)
    ISBN-13: 978-1-4104-3309-1 (hardcover)
    ISBN-10: 1-4104-3309-9 (hardcover)
    1. West Virginia—History—Civil War, 1861–1865—Fiction. 2. Large type books. I. Title.
PS3552.R2917M68 2010
813'.54—dc22   2010036999

Published in 2010 by arrangement with Barbour Publishing, Inc.

Printed in Mexico
1 2 3 4 5 6 7 14 13 12 11 10

AUTHOR'S NOTE

The herbs mentioned in this story were carefully researched and are authentic to the era. Some have since been found to be questionable or even dangerous. In no way do I advocate the use of any herb, medication, or curative without checking first with your medical doctor.

ONE

Wheeling, Virginia, 1861

Would the prospect of buying a new dress for the Fourth of July celebration compensate for all the drudgery and humiliation she had endured in this household?

As if Nancy Logan's thoughts had penetrated the ceiling into the bedroom above, her employer, Tabitha Clark, commanded from the top of the stairs, "Nancy, when Dr. Foster arrives, go to the door and ask him to come to Tommy's bedroom. And see that you greet him correctly."

Annoyed by her employer's tone, Nancy threw the feather duster on the floor and waited for the doctor's arrival. "A body's only got two hands and two feet," she muttered. "Nancy, do this. Nancy, do that," she said, mimicking her employer as she listened for a knock on the door.

In Nancy's opinion, Tommy didn't need a doctor. All the boy needed was a cup of mint tea and a poultice of lard and kerosene on his chest overnight. But Tommy's sniffles and shortness of breath provided a good excuse for Widow Clark to entertain the handsome young doctor who had come to Wheeling from Philadelphia a year ago. It was common knowledge that the widow was at least ten years older than Dr. Foster, but during the few weeks Nancy had worked in the Clark home, he had already come to see Tommy four times.

Nancy couldn't imagine why a smart man like the doctor couldn't figure out that Mrs. Clark was casting her net in his direction.

Nancy wouldn't mind having the doctor take notice of her, too, but she wouldn't pretend to be sick to snag his attention. *Though it would be nice if the good Lord would give him some reason to notice me,* she thought.

Several minutes passed before she heard a knock at the door. Mrs. Clark must have been watching for the doctor, for she alerted Nancy before he had time to get out of the buggy and tie his horse to the hitching post. Nancy straightened her white cap and dainty apron and forced a smile to her face.

"Come in, Doctor," she said, standing to one side and bowing as Tabitha had taught her to do.

Heath Foster stepped into the entrance hall, took off his hat, and handed it to her. "Good afternoon, Miss Logan."

Nancy hung his hat on the hall tree beside the door.

"Mrs. Clark wants you to come see Tommy right away. You know which room it is?"

"Yes, thank you."

Nancy watched as he walked up the stairway. On their first meeting, she had tagged the doctor as a compassionate person, which any man who wanted to be a doctor ought to be. And he was sure handsome, too! He wore his sandy-colored hair long, and it was thick and curled loosely around his nape. His face was lean and beardless except for the long sideburns. Dark brown eyes glimmered above his high-bridged nose. He was a man of medium height, so Nancy didn't have to crook her neck to look up at him like she did a lot of men.

Because she had been ordered to prepare tea to be served in the parlor before Dr. Foster left, Nancy went to the kitchen. Earlier in the day, she had set out the silver tray and shined it until she could see her face in it. Before she had left for her afternoon off, the cook had told Nancy how to prepare and serve the tea, but this was the first time Nancy had served in this capacity, and she was nervous about it.

She dropped another chunk of coal in the stove and moved the teakettle to the hottest part of the stovetop. While she waited for the water to heat, Nancy arranged slices of raisin bread and pound cake on a china plate. By the time she heard footsteps descending the stairs, she was ready. But she waited until she heard the soft *ding-a-ling* of a silver bell before she lifted the heavy tray, walked down the hall, and entered the parlor.

Keeping her eyes straight ahead, Nancy didn't see the duster she had earlier tossed on the floor, and she stumbled over it. The tray tilted in her hands, and the plate of bread and cake slid to the floor.

Jumping to his feet, the doctor took the tray out of Nancy's hands and placed it safely on the low table close to where Mrs. Clark sat. Nancy caught her balance and stood like a statue, staring at the food on the floor, knowing that if it hadn't been for Dr. Foster's quick thinking, the tea service would be there, too.

"Clumsy girl!" Mrs. Clark shrieked. Her mouth twisted in anger; her dark eyes were venomous. She pointed at the duster. "Not only clumsy but negligent, too! Can't you do anything right? Clean up this mess. Then get out of my house, and don't come back. You're fired!"

Nancy started shaking, and she felt blood rushing to her face. It was bad enough to be humiliated in front of Dr. Foster, whom she admired, but Mrs. Clark's words angered her. She jerked off the white apron and cap she was required to wear and dropped them on top of the bread and cake.

"Clean your own floor," Nancy said. She turned and rushed down the hall to the kitchen, grabbed her coat off the rack beside the back door, ran down the steps, and headed toward the alley behind the Clark home. Although it was April and the red-bud and dogwood trees were blooming on the hills surrounding Wheeling, the wind from the Ohio River was brisk and cold. But Nancy didn't take time to put on her coat, for she wanted to get away from the Clark home as quickly as possible.

At the end of the alley, she turned left on Main Street, wondering what she should do. Her Christian duty was to return to the Clark home and apologize for her behavior. But she just couldn't — especially if Dr. Foster should still be there.

She walked blindly, knowing that she must get over her anger before she went home.

11

Her father hadn't wanted her to work for Tabitha Clark in the first place. Mrs. Clark's brothers were his competitors in the steamboat business, and her father thought they looked down on him because he owned only *one* boat. He would cause a ruckus if she told him how the woman had talked to her.

Recalling her earlier thoughts, she muttered, "God, I wanted You to make something happen so the doctor would notice me. But did You have to go this far? I just expected a little miracle, not a thunderbolt."

Nancy didn't figure Heath Foster would forget her after what he'd seen and heard today. And the worst part of it was that she knew she was really at fault. She shouldn't have thrown that duster on the floor in the first place. Tears stung her eyes, and partially blinded by the bright sun, she stumbled along the streets of Wheeling with no particular destination in mind.

Mrs. Clark sat in silence for a few moments, her face more crimson than Nancy's had been, but she soon said angrily, "The nerve of that girl! Talking to me that way! It's impossible to find good help these days!"

Heath tried to think of some discreet way to make an exit from this embarrassing situation. At a loss for words, he knelt on the floor and started picking up the food and putting it on the tray.

"Stop!" Mrs. Clark said. "You're a guest in my house. I don't expect you to clean the floor."

Heath finished picking up the food, noticing that Mrs. Clark made no move to help him. He set the plate on the table. "I think I should go now. You're upset, and it's better for you to be alone. Let me know if the medication doesn't help Tommy."

"Oh," Mrs. Clark pleaded, "don't leave. Don't go without your tea."

"Thank you, but I rarely take time for tea. And I do have other calls to make."

She followed him to the door, wringing her hands, begging him to stay. But he bowed himself out of the house with as much grace as possible. When he reached the street, he hardly knew which way to turn, but he walked to the left, looking for Nancy Logan. He had noted the girl's distress, and he didn't think she should be alone.

When he reached Main Street, Heath saw her walking slowly, her head down. "Just a minute, Miss Logan," he called, and she turned to face him. "Are you all right?"

Surprise and anger lit up her eyes. A blush spread over her cheeks, and she looked away. "Yes, I'm all right," she answered, "but I'm mad."

"I gathered that," he said, smiling.

She kept walking, and he turned, matching his steps to hers.

"I have a call to make in this direction. May I keep you company?"

"I reckon," she said. "But I won't be good company. I should have listened to Pa. He didn't want me to go to work in that house. He said Mrs. Clark's family is too stingy to buy slaves — that they just hire white folks and treat them like slaves."

"Who is your father?"

"Wendell Logan. We live at the waterfront. Pa owns and operates the *Wetzel,* a packet boat."

"Oh yes, it runs from Wheeling to Parkersburg, I believe."

They were walking past the headquarters of the *Wheeling Intelligencer* when three newsboys catapulted from the building like shells spewed out of cannons.

"Extra! Extra! Read all about it!" they shouted as they extended papers toward everyone on the street.

"Here, boy," Heath called. "I want a paper."

He reached into his pocket and dropped some coins in the boy's hand. Nancy crowded close to him, and when he unfolded the paper, he held it so that she could see the headline: CONFEDERATE TROOPS FIRE ON FORT SUMTER. Shock and disbelief knotted Heath's stomach, and his voice trembled as he read the opening sentence aloud: "Today at 4:30 a.m., Confederate troops opened fire on Fort Sumter in Charleston Harbor."

He lifted his head and in an agonized voice cried out, "Oh God in heaven! Have mercy on us. Have mercy on us."

"But what does it mean?" Nancy stammered.

"It means war, child," he said. "It means war!" Crushing the paper in his hands, Heath turned from her and walked away.

Although she was stunned by Dr. Foster's troubled voice, Nancy looked sharply at him. Child! Did he consider her a child? She'd been doing the work of a woman since her mother had died. At eighteen, she hardly considered herself a child!

The newspaper office was located in the center of Wheeling's business section, and people poured out of stores and offices. The streets filled with people running back and forth. Some were shouting. Others laughed. Many women were crying. Nancy walked among them, trying to make sense out of what they were saying. She didn't know much about the current political unrest in the country, except that South Carolina had seceded from the United States of America in December. Much to her father's disgust, delegates were now meeting in Richmond to decide if Virginia, too, would leave the Union.

"Let 'em secede!" Wendell Logan had shouted. "People here west of the mountains will be better off without 'em. The western counties won't leave the Union."

"But Pa," Nancy had argued, "we have to be part of a state, don't we? What would we call ourselves?"

"Oh, I don't know," her father had said impatiently, for he was long on opinions but short on facts. "I reckon we can be part of Ohio."

As she wandered in and out of the excited throng, Nancy heard someone call her name, and she turned as her friend Stella Danford ran toward her.

"Oh, Nancy! Isn't this terrible?"

"Seems like that to me," Nancy agreed as she pulled Stella to one side. "But most of these people act like they're happy."

Tears ran down Stella's face, and she swiped at them with her hand. "I'm not

16

happy. Mama and Papa are talking about leaving Wheeling," she said. "Our kinfolks live in Alabama, and Mama wants to go home. I'm afraid."

Stella's words brought fear to Nancy's heart, too. Since she didn't think she would be affected one way or another, she hadn't paid much attention to the political discussions that had swirled around Wheeling like storm clouds the past few months. But this was serious. She and Stella went to the same church, and they had been friends since Stella's father had come to Wheeling to supervise the clothing factory his family owned. Nancy didn't want her friend to move away.

"What are you doing here by yourself?" Nancy asked.

"I heard all the shouting, and Mama sent me to find out what was going on."

"Everybody's talking at the same time, and I can't make much sense out of what they're saying. Let's walk down to the river where it's quieter."

Nancy shivered and realized that she was still carrying her coat. She put on the long woolen garment, buttoned it, and intertwined her arm with Stella's. They left Main Street and walked silently along the stone pavement of a side street. Two-story red brick houses with black chimney pots lined the street. Coal smoke from the chimneys filtered into Nancy's nostrils. As they walked, she told Stella about the flare-up at the Clark home.

"Mrs. Clark is one of Mama's friends. She's always so nice — I'm surprised that she treated you so mean."

"She's never shouted at me before, but she's always pushing me to do more work. I'm used to working, and I did what she said. I didn't have any choice, especially when I'm trying to make money to buy a dress with a hoop and everything that goes with it. Now I won't have a new dress."

"I'll let you have one of my dresses," Stella offered. "You could take the hem up to fit you."

While Nancy had always admired Stella's clothes, which the Danfords ordered from New Orleans, she wasn't tempted by the offer.

She shook her head. "Pa won't take charity. And he can't see any reason for a hoop skirt anyway. He said if I got one, I'd have to earn the money to buy it. And I don't have half of the money for the things I want."

"Do you need it for something special?"

"I'd like to have something new to wear

to the Fourth of July celebration." Looking in disfavor at her dark cotton homemade dress, she added, "Until I start wearing grown-up clothes, people will never realize I'm not a girl anymore." *Especially Heath Foster,* she thought.

"We have more than two months before Independence Day. Maybe you can find another job."

As they walked, Nancy wondered how her life would change if there was a war. Her father had come to Wheeling when he was a boy, and he had witnessed its growth from a sleepy Southern town to a thriving industrial city of more than fourteen thousand people. Virginia was the only place she had ever lived, and she couldn't imagine leaving. Of course, it was different with Stella's folks.

"I wish you wouldn't move," Nancy said, and Stella wiped tears from her eyes with a linen handkerchief.

"I don't want to leave you," she said, "but Papa says if there is a war, Southerners won't be welcome here. The western counties of Virginia are different from the rest of the state, and he doesn't think this area will pull away from the Union. He intends to leave before fighting starts."

"Your father is right. We do have more in

common with our neighboring states than we do with people east of the Allegheny Mountains or the states farther south."

They arrived at the riverfront and looked across a channel of the Ohio River to Wheeling Island. Nancy had learned as a child that in colonial days it had been called Zane Island after a family of early settlers in the area. Now a suspension bridge with abutments on the island spanned the water between the city of Wheeling and the state of Ohio.

Pointing to the small packet boat moored at the foot of Market Street, Stella said, "I see your father is at home. If we leave, I suppose we could travel partway with him." Sighing deeply, she continued, "I'd better go home. Mama will be worried about me and wondering what has happened. I didn't expect to be gone such a long time."

"I'll see you at church on Sunday," Nancy called as Stella ran down the bank to her home. Besides losing her best friend, she wondered in what other ways a war would change her life.

TWO

As she always did after a day at the Clark residence, Nancy compared her modest home to the splendor of her employer's. Because the area was prone to flooding, her family's living quarters were on the second floor of a frame house — ten feet above ground level. They had survived many floods when their neighbors, who lived in one-story houses, lost their homes. But when the Ohio overflowed its banks, her father kept a johnboat tied to the porch of the second floor in case they had to evacuate. It was scary sometimes when the muddy floodwaters completely surrounded their home, but Nancy had grown used to it, and her brother always took advantage of the situation by sitting on their front porch and catching catfish from the backwater.

Her father was working on a boat engine in his machine shop on the first floor of their home, which also served as a warehouse. Nancy called to him as she started up the steep steps to the left of the house.

"Supper will be ready before long, Pa." He nodded that he'd heard her.

Nancy stoked the fire and pulled the pot of rabbit stew she'd made that morning to the front of the stove. She hurried into her bedroom and took off her coat and washed her hands. The Logan living quarters consisted of three rooms. The combination kitchen and sitting room fronted toward the river. She had a small bedroom to herself, while her father and only brother, Clay, shared a room. Nancy hadn't realized what a simple home they had until she started working for Mrs. Clark, at whose home she had experienced a taste of gracious living.

Nancy ground coffee beans and put them in the coffeepot to make a hot drink for her menfolk. By that time, the oven was hot, and she sifted dry ingredients and added milk to make biscuits. After she cut the soft bread into large circles, she dabbed each piece in a pan of hot lard, placed them in an iron skillet, and put the biscuits in the oven to bake.

As she worked, Nancy's thoughts rioted with all the things that had happened that day. From the time she was a child, she had kept house for her brother and father. Year after year went by without many changes. If the country did go to war, what difference would that make in their lives?

Clay was five years older than Nancy. He had never liked working on the river and had angered his father three years ago when he quit the river to take a job as night watchman at the Merchants and Mechanics Bank. But Nancy was pleased when he started working at the bank, for he had generously contributed to the household needs, which made her life easier.

Supper was ready when her father came upstairs and took his place at the head of the table. At forty-five, Wendell Logan was a handsome, muscular man, and Nancy often wondered why he hadn't remarried. She hadn't asked him, because she sometimes found it difficult to talk to her father, although she and her brother could talk about anything.

Clay was usually out of bed by now, but apparently he was still asleep. So Nancy called him, and soon he entered the kitchen. He yawned widely and stretched his tall, lean frame, then pumped water into a pan and washed his face and hands.

As she usually did when she looked at her brother, Nancy wondered why she couldn't have been tall like the men in her family, instead of being short and petite like her mother. Rather than sharing their dark features, she despaired of her medium-brown hair, light complexion, and blue eyes.

Nancy spooned the stew into three bowls and placed a plate of biscuits on the wooden table. She added a jar of strawberry preserves and a bowl of butter. After Pa prayed, the family ate with a minimum of conversation. When her father finished, he pushed back his chair and sipped his second cup of coffee.

"Lots of excitement uptown today," he said. "What was going on?"

Since Clay had slept through the afternoon, both men turned to Nancy.

"The Confederates in South Carolina fired on Fort Sumter early this morning. The *Intelligencer* put out an extra."

"The news must have come over the wire in a hurry. Did you bring home a copy of the paper?" Clay asked.

"No. I left my reticule at Mrs. Clark's house and didn't have any coins," Nancy answered, remembering for the first time that she'd failed to pick up the reticule when she ran from the house. She had about a dollar's worth of coins in that bag, which she probably would never see again. She wouldn't risk the woman's anger by going back after her money. So, she thought glumly, she no longer had a job and she'd just lost a dollar of her hard-earned money. She might as well kiss the new dress and hoop good-bye.

"What else did you hear?" Clay demanded, interrupting her thoughts.

"A big crowd gathered right away, and I walked around to listen. There was a lot of arguing going on — some thinking the Confederates had done right, others cussing them because they'd started a war."

"And there ain't nuthin' worse than a civil war," Pa said. "But though I hate to think it, that little incident might just be the spark needed to spur the western part of this state to break away from Virginia. We don't have nuthin' in common with them slave owners in the East anyway."

"To my notion, South Carolina did the right thing," Clay said. "The North has been pushin' the South around long enough. The whole South ought to take up arms against the northern bullies."

Slapping the table with the palm of his hand, Pa shouted, "Son, as long as you're under my roof, you can keep your treasonous ideas to yourself. I ain't liftin' a hand agin' the United States of America, and I forbid you to. Your great grandpappy was killed at Saratoga fightin' the British to get us our freedom. I ain't about to give it away by joinin' a bunch of rich slaveholders who want to destroy this Union."

Perhaps Clay knew this wasn't the time to defy his father, for he didn't answer. His face paled, and he left the table and went to the bedroom. Nancy hurried to spread the leftover biscuits with jam and wash an apple to put in his dinner bucket. She handed it to him when he came back into the kitchen ready to go to work. His face was clouded with anger, but he took time to bend over and kiss Nancy's cheek.

Her father was angry, too, and Nancy decided not to mention her fracas with Tabitha Clark. She washed the dishes while he stalked around the room muttering under his breath.

"I'm going down to the river, Pa."

He waved his hand in dismissal. "Be back before dark."

She walked to the wharf where the *Wetzel* was tied up. She climbed to the top deck and sat on a bench. The sun, filtering through dark clouds on the western horizon, had turned the waters of the Ohio to crimson. She never got tired of this view.

On the eastern side of the valley, a range of high bluffs towered over the town. In the gathering dusk, she saw smoke from the factories that were located to the north and south of the business and residential areas. For the most part, the trees lining the streets were just beginning to leaf out, but the willow trees along the riverbank had been showing green for a month. Nancy loved her home during all seasons of the year, but she was most partial to it during the spring. It seemed as if God, knowing how dreary the long winter had been, wanted to give His people a special treat.

When the sun dropped behind the clouds, Nancy left the boat. As she neared her home, she became aware that a rider was approaching. She wasn't surprised to recognize Heath Foster, for he often visited patients in the evening. But she was surprised that he reined in the sorrel horse when he came abreast of her.

"Miss Logan, I told my mother that you might be looking for work. She needs help around the house, and since I had a call in this direction, I told her I'd let you know. If you're interested, go to see her when it's convenient for you."

For a moment, Nancy was speechless, then she mumbled, "Well, thank you! Thank you very much." The possibility of a fancy dress with a hoop loomed again in Nancy's future.

Heath touched the brim of his hat and rode on, leaving Nancy staring after him. In spite of the incident with Widow Clark and the possibility of war, the day had turned out well after all.

"He's sure takin' notice of me for some reason," she said softly.

But Nancy started upstairs with another problem. How was she going to explain to her father that she no longer worked for Tabitha Clark? And how would he feel about her going to work for the Fosters? They were Quakers, and Pa didn't hold with their religious views. How could she change his mind if he put his foot down and refused to let her work for Mrs. Foster?

THREE

Nancy knew she would have to downplay the incident or her father would storm over to Mrs. Clark's house and give her a bawling out that she wouldn't soon forget. Should she tell her father about Dr. Foster's offer? Or should she go and talk to Mrs. Foster first and then tell her father?

She had pleaded with Pa for weeks before he finally agreed that she could work for Mrs. Clark, and when she now told him how the woman had talked to her, he would throw a fit. But she had to tell him before he heard it from another source. Nancy knew she would have to downplay the incident or he would storm over and give Mrs. Clark a bawling out that she wouldn't soon forget.

When she heard the clock in the kitchen strike the hour of five, Nancy slipped out of bed, washed quickly, and put on her clothes. Her father expected his breakfast to be ready when he got up, and she didn't want him to be irritated this morning.

Nancy stirred the coals in the iron stove, laid wood chips on the coals, adjusted the damper on the stovepipe, and soon had a hot fire going. She had laid out the cutlery, pottery cups, and plates the night before. She quickly filled the coffeepot with water from the pitcher pump that brought water from the deep well behind their house. It was a sore spot with Pa that water lines hadn't been run to their street yet.

When the stove was hot, she mixed up a batch of biscuits and shoved them into the oven. She cut thick slices of ham and put them in a skillet. The coffee was hot when her father came from the bedroom. Everything was just the way he liked it, so he should be in a good mood.

"Mornin', Pa," she said in her brightest voice.

"Best of the day to you," he said. "That ham smells good."

She poured a mug of coffee and placed it beside her father when he sat down. "I'll get the milk while your coffee cools. The food is almost ready."

Nancy hustled downstairs to the cellar dug below the level of the first floor. The Logans bought milk and eggs three times a week from an Ohio farmer. When she came out of the cellar with a pitcher of milk, Nancy saw Clay approaching the house.

"You got breakfast ready, Sis? I'm starved."

"Just about."

"I'll wash up down here."

"No hurry. I've got to fry the eggs yet. How many do you want?"

"Three will be enough. That is, if you've got plenty of ham."

Nancy laughed over her shoulder at her brother as she hurried up the steps.

She set the pitcher beside her father. "How many eggs for you?"

"Two."

To Nancy's relief, the civil unrest in the country wasn't mentioned while they ate. As soon as Clay finished eating, he said, "I'm going fishing before I go to bed — maybe I can catch a string of catfish for supper."

Clay left the house, and while she removed his dishes from the table, Nancy heard him whistling as he headed toward the river. Waiting for her father to finish his breakfast, she looked out the window. The heavy fog on the Ohio when she had gotten up had lifted considerably, and the sun was breaking through the haze.

Her father finished the ham and biscuits on his plate, and Nancy refilled his coffee cup as he pushed back from the table with a satisfied look on his face. He always said that if a man had a good breakfast, he could make it through the day. If there was a good time to approach her father about something that would irritate him, this was it.

Nancy perched on the edge of her chair. Pa sipped on his coffee, a remote expression on his face. She wished she knew what he was thinking about. She opened her mouth twice before she could speak a word.

"Pa." Her voice trembled a little, and she wondered if her father noticed it. He turned his attention to her and waited. "Mrs. Clark fired me yesterday."

A frown spread across his features. "Go on," he prompted.

"She was entertaining Dr. Foster. I carried in the tea tray and stumbled, and the bread and cake fell on the floor. She said I was clumsy and ordered me to clean up the mess I'd made. I got mad and told her to clean it up herself."

One corner of Pa's mouth twisted upward into a grim smile.

"She fired me then, but I intended to quit regardless. I don't like to work for her."

Nancy expected him to say, "I told you

so." Instead he said, "Anything else I need to know before I pay Mrs. Clark a visit?"

"I stumbled over a duster I'd dropped on the floor when I went to the door to let the doctor in. So it was my fault, but I didn't like the way she hollered at me. I'd rather you don't say anything to her, but I don't suppose she'll pay me the money she owes me. And I left my reticule there with some coins in it."

Her father's expression grew serious, and Nancy waited breathlessly for his decision. Although his temper could be volatile at times, usually he deliberated before he took action. At length, the tense lines on his face relaxed.

"I'll bide my time on this," he said. "Since you were at fault and had the gumption to tell her off, that should be enough for now. But she *will* pay you what she owes you, and she'll return the bag and money." He turned a stern eye on his daughter. "Maybe this has taught you a lesson."

Nancy squirmed in her chair, and the beginning of a smile curved the corners of her mouth. "Not exactly."

"And what does that mean?"

"Dr. Foster stopped by last night and told me that his mother needs some help. I want to go see her today. I still need to earn some money for that new dress and hoop I've told you about."

A look of pure anger crossed Pa's face. He hit the table with the palm of his hand, which shook his cup and sloshed coffee on the table. He jumped to his feet and angrily strode around the room. "Why can't you be content with what you have? We have plenty to eat, a roof over our heads, and all the clothes we need. Why do you want to copy people who are better off than we are?"

Although her father's anger usually daunted her, Nancy held her ground.

"I don't know! That's just the way the good Lord made me. It's not just pretty clothes I want, but I want to learn things, too."

"I paid to send you to that female seminary for five years. You can read and write better'n I ever could."

Nancy struggled to maintain her determination. She knew instinctively that there was more at stake than the issue of working for Mrs. Foster. If she relented now, she could see the trend of her future. She would continue to keep house for her father until he decided it was time for her to marry, and he would choose her husband. Nancy realized that was the normal scheme of things for women, and perhaps it always would be, but she wasn't content to settle for the way things had always been if she could improve her circumstances. She wanted to earn some money. And she wanted to learn new things, for she'd had just enough education to realize how much more there was to know. And she wanted to choose the man she married — someone she could love.

She knew her father would scorn such romantic notions, so she said, "But I want to learn more. When I go to the library and check out a book, I see hundreds of books. How many books do we have in this house? One — the Bible. I want books I can call my own. I'd even like to have my own Bible. I don't like to be disobedient or defy you, Pa, but as long as I take care of you and the house, I don't see why I can't take time to do the things I want to do."

Surprisingly, amusement flickered in his eyes.

"Go right ahead, then. I never did think much of a woman who let a man run over her."

Nancy was stunned for an instant, finding it hard to believe that he had acquiesced so quickly. Then she galvanized into action and did something she hadn't done for years. She ran to her father, threw her arms around him, stood on tiptoe, and kissed his cheek.

"Thanks, Pa. I'll go see Mrs. Foster today."

"I'm warning you about one thing. I don't want you to be took in by the Fosters' religion. They're Quakers, and they have some farfetched ideas about what the Bible teaches. I ain't havin' my daughter spoutin' their heresy."

Nancy wasn't sure how the Quaker religion differed from her own, but she wouldn't argue the point now. She intended to follow up on her victory before he changed his mind.

He took some coins out of his pocket. "If you're goin' uptown this morning, bring home a newspaper. I want to see what Campbell has to say in the *Intelligencer* today. I don't like the way things are happenin' in this country. There's not much standin' between us and war."

Even the gloom on her father's face as he made this ominous prediction didn't dampen Nancy's anticipation of the day. She took extra care in washing the dishes and cleaning the house. Pa always put more fuel in the stove when he had a noon snack, so she put a pot of white beans on the back of the stove where they could simmer most of the day. She would make it a point to be home in time to fix the rest of his supper. Since he had been so nice about letting her work for Mrs. Foster, Nancy didn't intend to neglect him. She just hoped Mrs. Foster would like her work.

Nancy spruced up the kitchen as fast as she could. She carried a bowl of hot water into her bedroom and sponged her body, using a bar of honey-scented soap she'd bought at the store. Although she knew Mrs. Foster wouldn't see her underwear, she chose the best she had. She put on a linen chemise, a petticoat, and a pair of scarlet flannel drawers that came to her knees. She pulled the drawstrings tight around her slim waist before she stepped into her gray calico dress with a tight-fitting bodice and a gored skirt that flowed out gradually from her tiny waist to the wide hemline. She frowned at her image in the small mirror that hung over her dressing table. Her appearance didn't suit her, but it was the best she could do. Wrapping a white shawl around her shoulders, she hustled down the steps, paused at the shop door to call good-bye to her father, and headed uptown.

The Fosters lived in a modest, two-story, white frame house about halfway between the river and the high bluff behind the city. Nancy knew the location of the house, for she and Stella had walked by it more than once. Behind the house was a barn where Dr. Foster kept his two horses. A small building that had once been a garden house had been converted into his office. As Nancy approached the home, she wondered if she would see him today. She couldn't help wondering if her desire to work at the Fosters stemmed from a chance to make money to buy the dress or the opportunity to encounter the handsome doctor. She tried to put such confusing thoughts out of her mind as she walked up two steps to the porch and timidly knocked on the front door.

A tall woman with a gentle, wise countenance opened the door. She didn't bear any physical resemblance to Dr. Foster, so Nancy didn't know if she was his mother.

"I'm Nancy Logan. I came to see Mrs. Foster."

"I'm Hope Foster," she said in a soft and soothing voice and ushered Nancy into a small sitting room to the right of the entrance. "Sit down, Nancy. Would you like a cup of tea?"

"No, ma'am. I had my breakfast earlier, but thank you."

Nancy sat gingerly on the chair Mrs. Foster had indicated, thinking that she had never been offered refreshments in the Clark home and had never been allowed to sit anywhere except in the kitchen when the cook gave her a small lunch. She deduced that working for Mrs. Foster would be as different from working for Mrs. Clark as daylight was from dark.

In a quick glance she noted that her hostess's gray hair had been braided and wrapped around her head. A dainty white muslin cap sat on her head like a crown.

Sitting near Nancy, Mrs. Foster said, "My son tells me that you might have time to help with our housework."

"Yes, ma'am. I need to make some money."

"Tell me a little about yourself, Nancy."

"Did he tell you why I'm not working for Mrs. Clark?"

Mrs. Foster nodded, and her eyes seemed gentle and understanding.

"I live with my pa and brother on the riverfront. My mother died ten years ago when I was eight, and I've been doing for them since then. So I know how to do housework."

"I usually do my own work, but I've been having back problems. Heath wants me to slow down."

"I'd be glad of the chance to work for you. I could work a few days for free to see how you like my work. Mrs. Clark had me do a lot of things over — said I hadn't done them the right way."

A gracious smile overspread Mrs. Foster's face. "I'm sure that won't be necessary. It won't take long for you to learn how I want things done. Perhaps you can work for me four hours a day, three days a week. I could pay you thirty-five cents a day. Would that be satisfactory?"

Quickly Nancy calculated in her mind that she would make more than a dollar each week. She still had the better part of three months until Independence Day, which would allow plenty of time to accumulate enough money for the new dress and maybe some left over for other things.

"That sounds all right, but I'll have to ask Pa."

"Yes, of course. If he agrees, perhaps you could start day after tomorrow."

"Yes, ma'am." Nancy stood up because she didn't want to overstay her welcome. "If Pa doesn't like our arrangements, I'll come and tell you tomorrow. If he does, I'll come two days from now at nine o'clock."

Nancy had wanted to see the doctor, and

she glanced covertly at his office as she left the Foster home. She didn't see him, and in spite of her excitement over landing another job so quickly, she went home slightly disappointed.

FOUR

When her father gave his blessing to Nancy's new job, she spent the next day cleaning every nook and cranny of their home. It was a sunshiny day, and she washed the bed linens and hung them out to dry. She made loaves of wheat bread. She brought jars of green beans and hominy from the cellar to have handy if some days she was late getting home. But she intended to leave the Foster home every day in plenty of time to put Pa's food on the table when he was ready for it.

The next morning, calling good-bye to her father, she hurried up the bank, noting the activity up and down the river as she walked. A new steamboat was being built at the shipbuilding yard. A small tugboat was heading upriver toward Pittsburgh with a load of bleating sheep. At the wharf nearest the suspension bridge that spanned the Ohio, a dozen hogs were tearing into sacks of grain. As she watched, the harbormaster came storming out of the dock building and tried to run the hogs away from the cargo, but they were still there when the scene disappeared from Nancy's view. The hogs were a nuisance, but they kept garbage from accumulating on the streets, and when they grew too plentiful, city officials gave permission for residents to slaughter them for meat.

Nancy was all atremble as she approached the Foster home. What if she couldn't do the work to please Mrs. Foster? Pa had always taught her to do the best work possible no matter what she started to do, but the Fosters were bound to want things done in a different way from how she'd been taught. Mrs. Foster appeared to be a kind woman, but Pa had often cautioned her that looks could be deceiving.

When Nancy reached the Foster home, she stopped for a minute before she stepped up on the porch. Panic-stricken, she momentarily considered going back home and forgetting about a new dress. Maybe Pa was right in saying that she shouldn't want to live like people who were richer than the Logans. But a spark of determination ignited a renewed desire in Nancy's heart to better herself. She straightened her shoulders and walked confidently up on the porch, but when her hand shook as she knocked on the door, she knew she wasn't as confident as she wanted to believe she was.

Mrs. Foster must have been watching for her, because the door opened immediately.

"Come in, Nancy," she said with a smile. "Let me take your coat." She hung the coat on a hall tree. "Would you like a cup of tea before you start working?"

"No, thank you, ma'am."

"Then let me take you on a tour of the house." Perhaps sensing that Nancy was nervous, she continued, "I'm sure you and I will get along fine. I don't expect perfection in anyone. Don't worry about making mistakes. We all do that."

The Foster home was not as large as the Danford house, but as they went from room to room, Nancy decided that she liked it better than her own home. From the narrow entryway, they moved to a large parlor on the left, and behind it was Dr. Foster's bedroom, which they didn't enter. Across the hall was a commodious kitchen connected to a dining room, which opened into the small sitting room where Nancy had sat the first day she'd come to the house. Three bedrooms were located on the second floor, where Mrs. Foster slept.

"Since my son is often called out at night, we decided it would be more convenient for him to sleep on the ground floor. I'm rarely disturbed at night when he has to go out.

"So you see," Mrs. Foster said, "the house isn't large, and it won't be difficult for you to take care of it. I will clean Heath's bedroom, and it isn't necessary to clean the two spare bedrooms more than twice a month. It will be quite easy for you to dust, sweep, and mop the rest of the rooms during your working hours. I'll do the cooking. I would like to have your help with the laundry and ironing, but I won't overburden you with work. Do you have any questions?"

"Not yet, ma'am, but I'm sure I will."

"Then let's start today by having you clean the sitting room."

The next weeks passed in a daze of happiness for Nancy — she felt as if she entered a new world when she went inside the Foster home. Simplicity and peace marked the atmosphere of the household.

The Fosters had brought the furniture from their Philadelphia home. Furnishings in the parlor had belonged to Dr. Foster's maternal grandmother. Nancy particularly liked the Chippendale, serpentine-back, mahogany sofa with its cabriole legs ending in claw-and-ball feet. Two upholstered chairs with side wings, wooden legs, and hand rests were placed in opposite corners. A cabinet held pieces of glassware. Although wallpaper was not commonly used in Wheeling homes, the parlor wall was papered with historical scenes of the Revolutionary War. But the presence of peace and love exemplified in the home had the most effect on Nancy. She felt as if she was one of the family, rather than a servant.

Nancy sometimes fantasized that Mrs. Foster was her mother, and at times she felt that the older woman treated her like a daughter. A portrait of two young girls hung over the mantel in the sitting room, and Mrs. Foster told Nancy that her daughters, both older than Heath, had died within a week of each other, victims of an epidemic of smallpox that had swept through Philadelphia. She said that although Heath could barely remember his sisters, their deaths had prompted him to become a physician.

Dr. Foster usually took the noon meal with his mother, and Nancy was invited to eat with them. Often, when it was time for her to leave, he was ready to visit patients, and he would ask her to ride with him to the foot of the street or even to her own home if he had a patient to see along the river road.

Nancy's admiration of Dr. Foster increased daily, and although she was afraid to even think of such a thing, she occasionally wondered if he was interested in her, too. At those times, she always chided herself for having a foolish imagination. Why would an educated man like the doctor be interested in a nobody like her? Her mind cautioned her to stop thinking about him as anything more than a man who was kind to everyone, but her heart rebelled and went its willful way. To put such foolishness out of her mind, she sometimes wondered how often Dr. Foster called at the Clark home.

Mrs. Foster worked right along with Nancy, and although at first Nancy made several mistakes, she soon learned how the Fosters wanted their house to look. The most enjoyable part of Nancy's job was when she was asked to dust the bookcases. One day, she counted the books. The Fosters had more than two hundred of them. Having so many books at her fingertips was inconceivable to Nancy. And the Foster books weren't for show as the books in the Clark home had been. There was always an open book on the sitting-room table beside the chair where the doctor sat.

Nancy handled the books lovingly and carefully as if she was in contact with the greatest treasure in the world. Mrs. Foster must have noticed Nancy's interest in the books, for one day, she said, "You're welcome to borrow any of our books you would like."

"Oh, ma'am," Nancy protested, "I might damage them or lose them. Thank you kindly, but I don't think I ought to take any of them home."

"Books aren't any good unless they're read. Borrow one at a time, and if there's anything in the books you don't understand, Heath will be glad to explain the passages to you. He's read all of these books — some more than once. I've never read as much as Heath and my husband. I read magazines more than books."

Nancy first borrowed *Jane Eyre,* and because she loved the novel, when she returned it, she borrowed *The Scarlet Letter.* Since her goal, however, was to improve her mind as well as to be entertained, she sometimes chose Ralph Waldo Emerson's writings. The days passed swiftly for Nancy. Despite the civil unrest in the nation, she had never been so happy — her work was rewarding, and she was also adding to her small hoard of money.

One day when Mrs. Foster had to visit a sick friend, she told Nancy she could go home early. Dr. Foster was waiting for her in front of the house when she finished washing the dishes and putting them in the cupboard. Holding the reins in his left hand, he extended the other one to help Nancy into the buggy.

"I have a call out in the country," he said. "Do you want to ride along with me? I get weary of the city and enjoy getting away from it for a while. I thought you might like a change of scenery, too."

Nancy hesitated. Although the doctor never called her "child" anymore, she hadn't detected that he thought of her in any other way, and this invitation confirmed it. She understood that social customs were more relaxed in the Trans-Allegheny region than in the eastern cities; still, men didn't often ask single women to go places with them without a chaperone. But Pa hadn't made a fuss about her riding along with Dr. Foster in his buggy, and she figured he would have told her if he didn't approve.

"Sure! I'd like that — and Pa won't be expecting me home yet."

"If I could practice my profession by living in the country, I wouldn't live in a town." He pumped the reins, and the horse moved away from the sidewalk. "But a doctor needs patients, and it's necessary to settle in a city, where the population is centered."

By now, she felt comfortable enough in his presence to ask questions.

"Wouldn't there have been more patients in Philadelphia?"

He grinned sideways at her. "Yes, but a lot more doctors, too."

When he reached Main Street, Dr. Foster turned left.

"I'll travel out of town along the National Road."

The National Road had had a great influence on the growth of Wheeling. The road, which ran from Cumberland, Maryland, across the state of Virginia, had reached Wheeling in 1818 and now crossed over the suspension bridge into Ohio. Pa often hauled freight on the *Wetzel* that came in over the road.

Mrs. Clark was sitting on the porch when they passed her home, and it gave Nancy a heightened feeling of satisfaction for the woman who had fired her to see her riding in the doctor's buggy. He touched his hat to Mrs. Clark, but she stared at them without responding. Nancy didn't say anything, but she wondered if Dr. Foster was thinking of the time she'd dropped the food on the sitting-room floor. The incident was uppermost in her mind, and she felt a blush spread across her face. She sneaked a sideways glance at him, but he was keeping his eyes straight ahead.

Pedestrians crisscrossed the street without any notice, dogs raced from the alleys to bark at the doctor's horse, and they met a wide variety of vehicles and other riders on the street. He didn't speak again until they left the city behind them.

"But the real reason I left Philadelphia," he said, as if ten minutes hadn't passed since she'd asked the question, "was to find a slower pace so I can do what interests me the most. I'm fascinated by medical research. I want to find new medicines to treat diseases for which there aren't any known cures."

Nancy looked at him with heightened interest and respect. During her few weeks with the Fosters, she'd learned that they were compassionate people. Not only did Dr. Foster treat the sick, but Mrs. Foster spent a lot of her time visiting and helping bedridden adults in her neighborhood. Nancy had glanced through a pamphlet on the bookshelf, which indicated that throughout their history, Quakers had been known for their humanitarian activities of prison reform and the humane treatment of mental patients. She hadn't found anything that showed why her father objected to their religion until she read that the Quakers rejected war.

She turned her attention to Dr. Foster when he said, "I intend to visit residents of the western mountains to learn their folk medicines. That's one reason the current political situation distresses me. Now that Virginia has seceded from the Union, this area may become a battlefield. If so, it won't be safe to travel — even on peaceful pursuits."

"I'm worried about what's happening in our family, too," Nancy admitted. "Pa and Clay can't be together ten minutes before they start arguing about the war. I can't believe how our lives have changed in such a short time. Sometimes I can't sleep at night for fretting about it."

Heath looked at Nancy, conscious of her distress, longing to comfort this girl who was becoming more and more important to him. But he could find no words to reassure her when he was also disturbed over the evidences of war all around them. He drove in silence, thinking about the changes the war had already made in Wheeling.

In an effort to cut off supplies to the seceded states, Ohio had stopped eastward shipments over the B&O Railroad, which had caused a shortage of supplies in the city. A military camp had been set up on the island across from Nancy's home. Union sentiment in Wheeling was predominant, and Heath sensed that the state of Virginia wouldn't ignore such internal rebellion for long. United States flags waved throughout the city, and residents of any home that didn't fly the flag were subject to ridicule and harassment.

Nancy sighed, and her slender fingers twisted together. Her lips trembled, and Heath impulsively shifted the reins to his left hand. He laid his right hand over Nancy's stiff fingers and held them until he felt the lessening of her tension as her fingers relaxed.

They traveled the rest of the way to the farmhouse in silence.

After Dr. Foster secured his horse to a post, he helped Nancy step to the ground. She was perfectly capable of jumping out on her own, but she had come to enjoy the little niceties he showed her. For the most part, Clay and Pa took her work for granted. She had been impressed by Dr. Foster's courtesy toward his mother, and he treated Nancy in the same manner, always voicing his appreciation for what she did for his mother.

The little farm was located on a high knoll overlooking the Ohio River. While he went inside to see his patient, Nancy sat on the front porch and enjoyed the peace of the countryside. She watched a robin fly back and forth from her nest to the ground, where she looked for worms to feed her young. The bright-breasted bird would tilt her head toward the ground, listen, and hop to another location, until she finally found a worm. She then flew upward and disappeared into a clump of cedar trees growing between the barn and the residence.

Hens cackled in a log chicken house. A pig squealed occasionally. A flock of white ducks waddled up from the river, and a goat nibbled on the brambles growing near the garden fence. Enjoying the peace and tranquillity of this scene, Nancy found it hard to believe that war could ever touch their county. She looked southeastward. Although she couldn't see the mountains, she believed that even if war should come, they would serve as a barrier to keep the enemy from invading their territory.

Last night her father had read aloud from

the seventy-second Psalm. The third verse — "The mountains shall bring peace to the people, and the little hills, by righteousness" — had suggested to Nancy that the mountains might provide a barrier their enemies couldn't scale. Still looking toward the mountains, she wondered if they *could* provide some protection for the western counties.

Her reflections ceased when a woman accompanied Dr. Foster to the door.

"Let me know if your husband doesn't improve, and I'll make another call."

"Just a minute, Doctor," the woman said. She returned to the house and brought out a basket of eggs. "We don't have no money now, but I hope this will pay your bill."

"Thank you very much. I'll return the basket the next time I'm out this way," Heath said as graciously as if she had given him money for his services.

He put the eggs under the buggy seat, and Nancy said, "I'd better hold the basket on my lap. Otherwise, a lot of the eggs might break before we get back to town."

"Thank you — that will be best."

He took her arm and helped her into the buggy, and when she was settled, he handed the basket to her. Nancy waved good-bye to the woman on the porch, then took hold of the basket with both hands. She didn't ask what was wrong with the farmer, for she'd noticed that Dr. Foster never discussed his patients. But she'd also noticed that he often brought produce into the kitchen when he returned from patients who lived in the country.

Mrs. Foster was always pleased with the fresh farm produce, and once she had commented, "My husband owned a clothing factory in Philadelphia, and I'm thankful he left Heath and me reasonably well off. With our extra income, Heath can treat anyone who comes to him whether or not they are able to pay."

As they passed Washington Hall on their entrance into town, Nancy wondered how the decision made there a few weeks ago would change her future. Assuming that the Virginia referendum on secession would pass, delegates from several Virginia counties west of the Allegheny Mountains had met for a few days to discuss possible partition from Virginia. The formation of a separate state to be called New Virginia was becoming a possibility, although some delegates argued that it was unconstitutional for a new state to be formed within the jurisdiction of any other state. The convention had adjourned without taking action on a separate state, but the matter was widely discussed.

And while the counties of western Virginia delayed a decision about statehood, the twenty-third of May — the day set aside by the Virginia legislature for the referendum on the secession ordinance — loomed closer. The general opinion in town was that the majority of Virginia's legislators would favor secession.

"Do you think the western delegates will approve the secession amendment?" Nancy asked.

"Not a chance."

"Then what happens to the counties that are loyal to the Union? Pa says we ought to become a part of Ohio or Pennsylvania. Do you think that could happen?"

"I don't know, Nancy." A few times after she had started to work at the Foster home, Dr. Foster had called her Miss Logan or "child," but lately he'd been calling her by her given name. If he continued that, she wondered if she would dare to address him as Heath.

Instead of continuing toward his home, he turned toward the river. In a thoughtful voice, he said, "It troubles me that the delegates to the referendum convention are talking about statehood."

"How could that happen?"

"I'm not sure. But I'm convinced that Virginia won't lose a third of her counties without a fight. That's why I'm worried. If this situation turns into war, the major battles will no doubt be fought between Washington and Richmond. But the Union will be determined to keep the western Virginia counties loyal to them, and Virginia won't give them up willingly. We'll probably see our share of fighting."

When he slowed the buggy to a halt in front of her house, Nancy asked, "Are you sorry you left Philadelphia to come to Wheeling?"

His dark brown eyes studied Nancy's face for several moments, as if he were seeing her for the first time. A crimson flush spread across his dark skin, and Nancy blinked, feeling light-headed. She looked down and realized that her hands were gripping the rim of the basket until her knuckles were white.

Her mind reeled with confusion, and to relieve the tension building between them, she babbled, "Well, look at this! I'm still holding the basket. You should have stopped at your house with these eggs. I could have walked home."

"Take the eggs as my gift, please. I brought

eggs home two days ago, and I know Mother has all she needs."

He stepped from the buggy and took the basket of eggs. Nancy jumped to the ground before he could help her. She couldn't bear the touch of his hands at this moment.

"Thanks for taking me with you today," she stammered. "It was nice to get out of town for a while. And thanks for the eggs. We buy produce from a farmer west of the river, but he hasn't been regular in his deliveries since the governor of Ohio issued orders prohibiting trade with a state that's planning to leave the Union."

"Shall I carry them for you?"

Nancy grabbed the basket from his hand. She wanted to get away from the doctor and think over what had happened today — especially in the past few minutes.

"No, thanks. I'll put them in the cellar before I go upstairs."

She turned and walked away from him, but paused and looked over her shoulder when he said quietly, "Nancy."

She waited breathlessly for him to continue.

"I didn't answer your question. No, I'm not sorry I moved to Wheeling."

Nancy watched as he stepped into the buggy, lifted the reins, and directed the horse away from her home. What was the meaning behind Dr. Foster's words and the slight smile lurking behind his mask of uncertainty? What impact would this moment they had shared have on her future?

FIVE

A few weeks later, the doctor came into the house just as Nancy finished her work and was putting on her coat to leave.

"Dr. Foster, do you mind if I take one of your Shakespeare books home with me? Your mother told me to borrow any of the books I wanted, but I notice that you read Shakespeare's works a lot, and I don't want to take anything you might want."

Nancy wondered about the expression that spread across his face. Was it humor, compassion, or adoration she detected in his eyes? Or a combination of all three?

"My dear Nancy," he said, "you can borrow any of the books you want to." She started to thank him, but he held up his hand. "On one condition."

"Oh!" she said, hardly knowing how to respond to his change in manner and the softness of his voice. Her lashes fluttered over her eyes momentarily, but she glanced up again as he continued.

"You can borrow any of the books you want to," he repeated, adding, "that is, if you'll stop addressing me as Dr. Foster and use my Christian name. It's Heath, you know."

Nancy lowered her gaze in confusion, and she felt a blush spread over her face. Her pulse seemed to be spinning out of control. But she sensed a peace and satisfaction she'd never experienced. She would have to wait until she was by herself to assess what had happened to her, but believing that she was on the brink of a closer relationship with Heath, she was determined to take advantage of it.

Her eyes searched his face for a few moments before she said bravely, "Yes, I know that's your name, and I've wanted to say it for weeks, Heath."

An eager look flashed in his eyes, and he stepped closer to her just as the back door slammed. With a feeling of frustration, Nancy knew that Mrs. Foster had returned from her errand.

When Mrs. Foster entered the room, Nancy was lifting a book from the shelves, and Heath was putting on his coat. "Mother, I'm going to walk downtown with Nancy to get a copy of the *Intelligencer*. I'll be back soon if anyone needs me."

Nancy said good-bye to Mrs. Foster without looking at her. When they stepped off the porch, she didn't know what she should say after that emotional scene between them, and perhaps Heath was also jolted out of his normal calmness, for they walked in silence to the newspaper office.

The situation in Wheeling had been tense since an overwhelming majority of local votes were cast against the secession ordinance, and Heath waited anxiously for each issue of the newspaper. Only eighty-seven citizens had voted for secession, which caused local residents to eye one another with suspicion.

"Have any more Confederate sympathizers had trouble?" Nancy asked when they stopped in front of the newspaper office.

Heath shook his head. "There have been many demonstrations in front of the homes of secessionists, but since Mr. Campbell denounced those activities as mob rule in his newspaper, there hasn't been any more overt harassment."

"I'm upset about my friend Stella. Their house has been pelted with mud, rotten eggs, and vegetables, so Mr. Danford is afraid for Stella and his wife. He has closed his clothing factory, and they're leaving tomorrow with Pa on the *Wetzel*. Their home is in Alabama."

Heath's eyes registered concern. "I'd heard they were leaving, and I'm concerned for them, too. That's a long trip, and they'll be traveling through hostile country part of the way."

Nodding, Nancy said, "Yes, but he's willing to risk that rather than to stay here and endure insults or danger to his family."

"I can understand his reasoning."

The war was never discussed within the Foster household, and Nancy voiced a question that had worried her for days.

"Are you going to join one of the militia groups?"

Heath gazed at her, surprise on his face. "Why, no! Quakers believe in nonviolence. I've dedicated my life to saving life — not killing people on the battlefield. I won't fight on either side. I assumed you knew that."

In a meek, quiet voice, she said, "I'm sorry. I had read that in a pamphlet at your house, but I'd forgotten. Excuse me for asking."

"You're welcome to ask me anything, Nancy — you should know that by now."

Momentarily, she was happy knowing that Heath wouldn't be going off to fight, but unease gnawed at her satisfaction. The majority of local citizens were living in euphoria because of the new state movement, so how would they react to a man who wouldn't fight on either side? Although he knew it meant war, her father had embraced the idea of a new, pro-Union state with patriotic fervor. She didn't think he would allow her to work for the Fosters if Heath made it public that he wouldn't fight to defend the Union.

Heath put his fingers under Nancy's chin and lifted her face.

"Look at me," Heath demanded.

She lifted her gaze to study his face. His dark eyes narrowed speculatively, searching her face as if he was trying to reach into her mind.

"Do you think I'm a coward — afraid to fight?"

She hesitated momentarily. She didn't think he was a coward, but she couldn't bear for other people to say that he was.

"No, I don't believe that for a minute."

He squeezed her chin gently and released her.

"Violence never solves anything," he said as they leaned against the building that housed the newspaper's offices. "Don't you remember what Jesus said when one of His disciples tried to defend Him with the sword? 'Put up again thy sword into his place: for all they that take the sword shall perish with the sword.' "

Nancy sensed the struggle Heath was having with his conscience, and she put her hand on his arm, hoping that her action would convey to him that whatever decision he made would seem right to her.

"My soul is burdened when I think of all the bloodshed that may occur before this war ends," Heath continued, and Nancy listened with rising dismay. "It's my opinion that thousands of men will be killed, maimed, and ruined during this conflict. I read a prediction this week that it might take four or five years before the Union can win the war. Four or five years! A generation of men could be wiped out. I find it hard to believe that people are rejoicing — rejoicing, mind you — that we are going to war. Why can't they understand what war will do to this nation?"

Several newsboys raced from the newspaper headquarters with the latest issue of the *Intelligencer,* and Heath bought a paper.

"I want one, too," Nancy called to a newsboy. To Heath she explained, "Pa gave me the money. He reads every word of it."

She tucked the newspaper under her arm.

"I have to go home now. Pa is heading downriver in the morning, and he'll want to read the paper before he leaves."

"How long is he gone on these jaunts?"

"He goes as far as Parkersburg, and his return depends on how much freight he hauls, the number of passengers, and the depth and current of the water. He can make the trip in three days, but sometimes it's longer than that."

"And your brother works at night? You stay alone?"

"I always have," Nancy said, shrugging her shoulders. "I'm not afraid."

She turned away from Heath, called goodbye, and started home. She would have to hurry to have the meal on the table.

After supper, Pa returned to the *Wetzel* for last-minute preparations, leaving Clay and Nancy together at the table. He fiddled with his coffee cup, and Nancy, knowing her brother well, waited. He had something on his mind, and like his father, he wouldn't speak until he was ready. Habitually, Nancy spoke up when she had something to say, a trait she had apparently inherited from her mother. She took the last piece of corn bread and spread it with butter. She ate slowly, dreading to hear what Clay had to say.

Through the open windows, she monitored the everyday sounds around their home. On the evening air, a bugle call wafted from the military camp on the island. A towboat passed downriver, and the captain greeted the crew of the *Wetzel* with three loud blasts of the whistle. A wren perched in a nearby maple tree, and its rich, whistled notes, which sounded alternately like *sweetheart, sweetheart* or *teakettle, teakettle,* invaded the quiet room. These ordinary happenings should have heralded that all was right in their community, but Nancy knew better. Watching the play of emotions on her brother's face, she felt a wretchedness of mind she had never experienced before.

"Sis," he said at last, "sometimes a man has to follow his conscience, no matter how much it hurts other people." He took a deep breath. "I'm leaving tonight. My friend Alex is going with me. We're aimin' to join the Confederate Army."

A soft gasp escaped Nancy's lips, and her body stiffened in shock. Although she had known that such an action was a possibility, when she heard the stark, bald truth from Clay's lips, the horrible results of a civil war hit home.

Brother against brother! Father against son!

Clay bolted out of his chair, knelt beside her, and put his arm around her shaking shoulders.

"I'm sorry, Nancy, but I couldn't think of an easy way to tell you."

"What's Pa going to say?"

"Nuthin' I want to hear. That's why I'm leaving without tellin' him." He pulled an envelope from his pocket. "If I tell him to his face, we'll both say things better left unsaid. But I'm not leavin' it up to you to tell him. I've spent most of the day writin' a letter to him. Don't give it to him until mornin'. By that time, I'll be a long way off."

"But your job?"

"I quit yesterday."

Tears blinded Nancy's eyes and choked her voice, but she gulped, "Clay, please don't go. What are we going to do after you're gone?"

"I have to go. I'm an able-bodied young man. We're at war, and I'll have to fight on one side or the other. If I don't fight, people will call me a coward. I have to choose sides, and I believe the South is right. I don't hold with slavery, but every state ought to have the right to do as it wants to do. If the

North makes the rebel states stay in the Union, that's just another kind of slavery. A man has to do what he has to do."

Nancy sat as if turned to stone while Clay went into the bedroom and returned with a bulging haversack. "I raided your bread box and cellar and took enough food to last us several days. We've heard that there's a Confederate Army as close as Barbour County, and we're headin' in that direction."

Clay continued to talk of his plans, but Nancy's mind was so numbed that she missed most of what he said. She only knew that he was leaving to fight with the enemy, but it was difficult to think of people in eastern Virginia or the Carolinas as enemies.

Dear God, what is going to happen to us? How will Pa react to his son's treason? And what about Heath? Will people think he's a coward? Will he be harassed?

Clay stopped beside Nancy, and she stood to put her arms around his waist. Tears glistened in his eyes, and she knew this hadn't been an easy decision for him.

"God bless you, brother. I'll pray for you every day."

As his steps receded into the distance, Nancy wondered if she would ever see him again. Her father wouldn't take his son's treason lightly. If Clay survived the war, she doubted he would be welcomed home.

Taking the sealed envelope with her, Nancy went into her bedroom and closed the door. As upset as she was, if she encountered her father tonight, he'd be sure to notice that something was wrong. She pulled a chair close to the window and wrapped a blanket around her shoulders. The wind off the river was cool, but Nancy's nerves were atwitter, which, rather than the cold air, probably accounted for the trembling of her body.

When she heard her father come into the house and go into his room, she undressed and got into bed, savoring the comfort of the feather tick as it closed around her. She dozed intermittently during the night, but at first light, she got up and made breakfast preparations. A sense of desolation swept over Nancy as she laid only two table settings. She kept Clay's letter in her pocket. She wouldn't give it to her father until he'd finished his breakfast.

She cooked a pot of oatmeal and raisins and had a large bowl of it by Pa's plate when he came into the kitchen. He greeted her briefly as he always did. He took no notice of Clay's vacant chair, for Clay didn't always come straight home after he left the bank. When he finished eating, Nancy refilled his coffee cup and laid the letter beside his plate.

She felt his questioning eyes on her, but she refused to meet his gaze. She crossed the room and stared out the window with unseeing eyes. She couldn't watch her father's expression when he read the news that would break his heart. Despite their differences, she had never doubted that a strong sense of respect and affection existed between father and son. The heavy silence in the room seemed as loud as a clap of thunder. Nancy realized that she was clenching her hands and her nails were cutting into her flesh. She relaxed her fingers.

After clearing his throat, Pa said huskily, "Have you read this?"

She turned toward him and shook her head.

"Then read it and burn it. He's a traitor to his country, but I won't turn him in."

"He's only doing what he thinks is right."

Her father lifted himself wearily from the chair, and he looked as if he had aged ten years. "I know, but he's brought shame upon the family. Don't mention his name to me again."

"But Pa . . ."

"I no longer have a son — you don't have

a brother. With the strong Union feelings in this town, he couldn't come home if I wanted him to. Forget him."

He went into the bedroom and closed the door.

She snatched up the letter and read the brief message:

Dear Pa,

I don't want you to hate me, but I can't set around and watch the country go to the dogs without tryin' to help. I know you will think I joined the wrong army, but I have to do what's right for me. Please pray for me and try to forgive.

Your lovin' son,
Clay

Tears nearly blinded Nancy, but she read the message again before she lifted the stove lid and dropped the letter on the hot coals. As she watched it burn, she said good-bye to her beloved brother. Automatically, she cleared the table and washed the dishes. She was hanging the dishcloth and towels behind the stove to dry when the bedroom door opened and her father leaned against the jamb. Whether he was enraged or mournful about Clay's decision, her father seemed to have conquered his emotions.

"I don't know what to do about you," he said. "You can't stay here alone while I'm away on the *Wetzel.*"

"But Clay was hardly ever home at night! Nothing has changed."

Pa shook his head. "Everything has changed. There's an army camp on the island. Mobs are threatenin' people all over the county. When word gets around that Clay has joined the Confederates, we might have trouble. And I hear a Union army is coming here from Ohio. I can't leave you alone."

"I could stay with one of the neighbors at night."

He continued as if she hadn't spoken. "The trouble is, I don't have much room on the *Wetzel* this time, or I'd take you with me. The Danfords are takin' a lot of boxes and suitcases with them."

"I want to see them off. I told Mrs. Foster I wouldn't come to work until the boat left."

"Do you suppose she'd let you stay with her at night while I'm gone?"

Surprised that her father had made this suggestion when he hadn't wanted her to work for the Fosters, Nancy said slowly, "She probably would. She's good to me, and I like her. They have two spare bedrooms."

"I don't have time to get somebody to stay with you this time, but I'll delay leavin' until I get you settled. I'll tell the crew that we may be a little late but to have everything ready when I get back."

Nancy had to trot a few times to keep up with her long-legged father as they walked to the Foster home. Nancy always opened the door and went in, but when they arrived at the house, Pa strode up the steps and knocked. Heath came to the door. He glanced from father to daughter quickly before he said, "Come in."

"No," Pa said. "I ain't got time for that. My son is away from home, and I'm ready to leave on my weekly trip to Parkersburg. I don't want to leave Nancy alone while I'm gone. I wonder if your mother would let her stay here. I'll come up with some other plans before my next trip."

"Why, I'm sure that will be all right. Just a minute." He turned and called, "Mother, will you come here, please?"

Mrs. Foster soon appeared at the door. Nancy watched her father size her up one side and down the other. Seemingly satisfied, he repeated what he had said to Heath.

"I'd love to have Nancy's company," Mrs. Foster said, and no one could doubt her sincerity. "She can stay here as often and as long as she wants to anytime. You won't have to make other arrangements."

"Just the nights I'm out on the boat. I'll pay."

"But that isn't necessary —"

Pa raised a hand to interrupt her. "If I don't pay, she don't stay."

Mrs. Foster smiled. "I'm sure we can agree on a reasonable rate for her keep." She turned to Nancy, "Are you staying now?"

"No, ma'am. I want to go back and say good-bye to Stella. She's leaving on Pa's boat. I'll be back after that."

"Bring what you need for a few nights. We'll be glad to have you."

Nancy had a feeling that Heath was watching her, and she slid a glance in his direction. She thought she detected approval in his eyes. She wondered briefly how it would seem to be a part of the Foster household.

Her father shook hands with the Fosters and shepherded Nancy off the porch. She looked back over her shoulder and waved to them.

An hour later, she stood on the dock waving good-bye to Stella and the rest of the Danfords as the *Wetzel* slipped away from the dock and accessed the deep channel of the river. To lose her best friend and her brother in such a short time was heart wrenching. She was thankful she wouldn't have to stay alone in the house for the next two nights.

By the time she was ready to leave for the Fosters, it was noon, so Nancy put jam on a biscuit and ate as she hurried uptown. She was heartbroken over the loss of Clay and Stella, but her heart rejoiced that, for a short time, she would be a part of Heath's family life.

Six

Heath had occasionally joined Nancy and his mother for the noon meal, which they ate in the kitchen, but she had known that the Fosters ate their evening meal in the dining room. Since she was a paid servant, Nancy wondered if she would be invited to share the evening meal with them or if she would still sit in the kitchen.

Mrs. Foster assigned Nancy the task of cleaning the three upstairs bedrooms. The room Nancy was to regard as her own, according to Mrs. Foster, was a small dormer room. The furniture was made of rosewood and had deeply cut, spiral-turned legs. The dresser had a white marble top. The high-backed bed and dresser filled up most of the floor space. Nancy had always admired the patchwork quilt made with patterned silk fabrics, one that Mrs. Foster had made when she was a girl.

Nancy had learned that the Fosters always

"dressed" for their evening meal, and just in case she was asked to join them, she had brought her church clothes — a white linen dress with a short dark blue jacket — that Clay had bought for her last birthday. She hung her garments on the clothes tree and tried to smooth out the wrinkles with her fingers.

When she went downstairs after cleaning the bedrooms to her satisfaction, Nancy walked through the dining room on her way to the kitchen. Three place settings had been laid at the table. She smiled, and her heart lifted. Her dismay at Clay's leaving lessened a degree.

Nancy was acutely aware of the differences in her family background and Heath's when she sat at the dining-room table and compared it to her own home. The table was covered with a linen cloth, several pieces of silverware surrounded the china plate before her, and a sparkling crystal glass was filled with water. Lighted candelabra shed a rosy glow over the table.

Heath sat at the head of the table and prayed before he served the food. Nancy was given the first portions as if she was an honored guest instead of a servant. He laid a thick slice of roast pork on her plate. "Would you like a larger serving of meat?"

"No, thank you."

"Please ask for seconds if you want more," he said as he put a dollop of potatoes on her plate and covered them with a thin layer of creamy gravy. He spooned a portion of his mother's pepper relish beside a slice of wheat bread that Mrs. Foster had baked in the afternoon. He passed the plate to Nancy and turned to his mother.

"How large a portion dost thou want?"

"The same size portion as thou gave Nancy will be fine, but not quite as many potatoes, please."

Throughout the meal, Nancy noticed, as she had before, that when Heath or Mrs. Foster spoke to her, they used the pronoun *you.* It was only when they addressed each other that they used the words *thee* and *thou.*

While Nancy washed the dishes that Mrs. Foster then dried and put in the cupboard, she said, "I've often wondered why you and Dr. Foster don't use *you* when you're talking to each other."

Mrs. Foster laughed softly. "The words *thee* and *thou* were used in earlier times. You will have noticed these words in the Bible."

"Yes, I remember that the Bible has those words, like when Jesus said, 'Thou shalt love thy neighbour as thyself.' "

"Some Quakers use the old pronouns when they're talking to other members of their faith or when they're speaking to members of their immediate family. They're also used as a term of endearment by sweethearts or between man and wife."

"I suppose I ask too many questions."

"And how else would you learn new things if you didn't have an inquiring mind! You may ask me anything you like."

Mrs. Foster took off her apron. "It's too early to go to bed, so you may join Heath in the sitting room." She picked up a plate she had filled with food and wrapped in a warm cloth. "I'm going to take supper to my neighbor down the street. I'll be back soon."

Nancy went down the hall and timorously entered the sitting room. Heath sat in a chair close to a light, reading, and she wondered if he would resent her presence. He looked up and smiled.

"Come in and find a comfortable place to sit. Mother says you like to read, so choose any book you like from the shelf."

Nancy took *Uncle Tom's Cabin* from the bookcase. She had noticed the book several times when she was dusting. She wanted to read it because an article in the *Intelligencer* had referred to the book as a cause of the war. She bypassed the chair where Mrs. Foster sat when she was reading or sewing and sat on the couch opposite Heath. He stood up and brought a lamp from the mantel and placed it where the light would fall on the open pages of her book.

He started to return to his chair but stopped when a knock sounded at the front door. Nancy thought he was probably being summoned on a sick call, and she was disappointed because she had looked forward to spending the evening with him.

Heath opened the door. "Good evening, Richard," he said. "How nice of you to stop by. Come in. Mother will be back soon."

A robust man past middle age entered the room, and Heath said, "Richard, this is Nancy Logan, who's staying with us a few days while her father and brother are away. Nancy, this is our neighbor Richard Donovan."

The visitor gave Nancy a brief smile while Heath pulled a rocking chair into the circle of light and invited him to be seated. "May I take your hat?"

Mr. Donovan shook his head, seated himself, and twisted his hat around and around in his hands. Heath took the book he'd been reading out of his chair, laid it aside, and sat down.

"What can I do for you?"

The visitor swallowed a few times. "This isn't an easy errand for me, Heath. But my mind is troubled, for we've been friends since you moved to Wheeling. I need to ask you some questions. I've denied some things I've heard about you over the past few days, and I want to set my mind at ease." Mr. Donovan looked at Nancy. "It might be better if we were alone."

The tension in the room was overpowering, and half rising off the davenport, Nancy murmured, "I'll go upstairs."

"Not unless you want to," Heath said.

She knew instinctively that Mr. Donovan wasn't the bearer of good news, and she didn't want Heath to hear it alone. She eased back on the couch and laid her book aside.

Donovan squirmed in his chair, but he took a quick breath and looked directly at Heath. "I've heard that you've been asked more than once to join one of the military companies forming in town and that you've refused."

"That's true," Heath answered without further explanation, and his mouth spread into a thin-lipped smile.

"I can't believe it!" Donovan said. "Does this mean you're a secessionist? Are you going to fight with the Confederates?"

Nancy had considered Heath one of the calmest men she'd ever known, but she saw a muscle contract in his jaw and sudden anger light his eyes. His voice was strained when he spoke. "We *have* been friends for a long time, and I pray that we can continue that friendship. Therefore, I'll answer your question. I'm a loyal Union man. I do not like slavery, nor do I respect the hotheads who have pulled this country into war. I have already signed the oath of allegiance to the United States of America. But . . ."

He paused, and his words were slow and distinct when he continued. "I will not join a militia. I will not go into the army. In an extreme case, I would consider violence. If someone should break into this house tonight and threaten Mother or Nancy, I would meet violence with violence. But I've dedicated my life to healing, not killing, and I will not enlist in the army. Before this conflict is over, doctors are going to be needed as much as soldiers. The people of Wheeling may be glad to have a resident doctor."

Donovan stood. "I guess I've heard what I came to find out. I suppose you have to live with your conscience, and I won't let your decision come between us as friends. But I think I should warn you that you and your mother may be in danger. Please be careful."

Heath closed the door behind his visitor and returned to his chair with dragging steps. He sat down and lowered his head into his hands. Nancy sat as if she'd been turned to stone. She longed to comfort him, but what could she do? What could she say?

After several minutes, she knelt beside Heath's chair, but she didn't touch him.

"I'm sorry," she whispered.

He looked up as if he'd forgotten she was in the room.

"Let's not mention this visit to my mother, please. She will hear soon enough. I've been getting the cold shoulder from several men the past few days, so I knew what to expect." He smiled wistfully in her direction. "Do you think any less of me than you did a few hours ago?"

She briefly touched his hand that lay on the arm of the chair and shook her head violently. "No, this hasn't changed my opinion of you at all. A man has to do what he has to do. My brother said that to me last night about this time."

His eyes questioned her.

"I guess it's time to tell you why Pa wished my company on you. My brother left last night to volunteer in the Confederate Army. Pa's afraid to leave me alone while he makes his run to Parkersburg and back. He figured I'd be safer with your mother."

"I'm not sure you're any safer here, but you heard what I said. I'll protect Mother and you with my life, if necessary, but I can't willingly take a man's life. I hope you understand."

The back door opened, and Nancy knew Mrs. Foster had returned. She jumped up from the floor and hurried to the couch.

"No matter what decision you make, I know it's the right one," she whispered. His glowing eyes thanked her.

SEVEN

The next few weeks were like a nightmare to Nancy. She couldn't believe that her life had changed so drastically in such a short time. Vigilantes roamed through the northern panhandle of the state, carrying United States flags, threatening death to all who refused to salute the banner. In Wheeling, the lines between secessionists and pro-Union adherents had been finely drawn. The news spread quickly that Clay Logan had joined the Confederates, and in spite of the fact that her father flew the national flag on the *Wetzel* and from the roof of their home, one night a group of masked men surrounded the Logan house, shouting invectives and calling for death to all traitors. Pa didn't go to bed all night. He stood at the door, his rifle ready to shoot the first man who put a foot on the steps to their living quarters. Nancy went to bed, but she didn't sleep.

The attackers withdrew a few hours before daybreak. When Nancy went to the kitchen, her father had already stoked the fire and had a pot of coffee perking. He sat at the table, his head in his hands.

"Did you sleep at all, Pa?"

He lifted bloodshot, worried eyes and shook his head.

"What are we going to do?"

"Not much we can do but wait it out and pray that these hoodlums get tired of their meanness. They're a bunch of no-gooders who've found an excuse to cause trouble. We'd be better off in the hands of the Confederates, at least as long as they're headed by General Lee. He won't put up with such carrying-on."

He stood and stretched as if his muscles had locked during the stressful night he'd spent protecting his home and his daughter.

"I'll fix your breakfast right away."

"I've tried to find some woman who would come in and stay with you when I take the boat out, but I can't find anyone. We'll have to impose on the Fosters awhile longer."

"Mrs. Foster doesn't mind, Pa — really she doesn't. She's good to me — treats me like family."

"Fact is," Pa said as he poured hot water

into a tin wash pan, stood in front of a mirror on the wall, and started shaving, "I'm not sure you're any safer there than you are at home. If Doc Foster won't sign a paper refusing to give aid to Confederate sympathizers, he's bound to be bullied, too."

"I heard him tell his mother that he took an oath to never turn away anyone who needed help, and he intends to doctor anyone who comes to him and not question that person's political beliefs. He's also being ridiculed because he won't join the local militias."

"And I hold that agin' him," her father said, his eyes hard as agates. "Time comes when a man has to fight!"

"From what I've overheard, he would fight to protect his mother and others who are weak, but he won't go to war."

Her father shook his head. "I don't expect you to soak up any of their heathen doctrine. Even our Lord oncet took up the whip and drove the money changers out of the temple."

Nancy didn't argue any more — her father had enough on his mind now without adding a rebellious daughter to his problems.

"I'm gonna walk with you to the Fosters' this morning, and I aim to stop by Widow Clark's and get that money she owes you.

You're goin' with me."

Although she dreaded facing Tabitha Clark, when her father used that tone, Nancy knew it was useless to argue with him.

As they hurried along the streets to the Clark home, Nancy wondered if her father had heard the rumors that Mrs. Clark had been spreading. Last Sunday at church, one of the women had pulled Nancy aside and whispered, "I don't like to spread gossip, but I thought I ought to tell you what Mrs. Clark is tattlin' around town. She's sayin' that you've been stayin' with the Fosters because you want to be near the doctor. And she's also tellin' what a poor worker you are, and that Mrs. Foster's only keepin' you on because she feels sorry for you."

That information had alarmed Nancy so much that she had nearly passed out, wondering what her father would do if he heard the tittle-tattle, too. But why, when he'd let weeks pass and hadn't confronted Tabitha Clark, had Pa taken a sudden notion to see the woman? Nancy's steps lagged behind her father's. If Mrs. Foster learned what was being said, would she lose her job? With a sense of dread, she figured she would soon have an answer to all of her questions.

Nancy stood half hidden behind her father

when he pounded on the front door of the Clark home. Nancy wondered who would answer their knock. Had Mrs. Clark replaced her?

Tommy opened the door. "Hi, Nancy," he said, and she smiled at him. She'd always gotten along fine with Tommy.

"I want to talk to your mother," Pa said.

Tommy ran toward the rear of the house, and Mrs. Clark soon strolled down the hallway. Pa stepped aside so that Nancy was no longer hidden. Mrs. Clark stopped suddenly, and a cold expression settled on her face.

"What are you doing here?" she said. "I told you not to come into this house again."

"She's not comin' in the house, but I will if you don't give me the four dollars she earned workin' for you, which you didn't pay, *and* the bag she left behind when you kicked her out."

"As clumsy as she was, she cost me more than four dollars by breaking some of my china."

"Get the money," Pa demanded and stepped inside the hallway.

Mrs. Clark turned on her heel, and with her back as rigid as a post, she walked toward the kitchen. Tommy crawled up on the stairs and looked as if he was going to cry. In a few minutes, Mrs. Clark returned. She threw Nancy's reticule and four gold dollars on the floor at Pa's feet. "Now get out of my house."

"I'm not finished yet. Count the money in your bag, Nancy, and be sure it's all there." When Nancy knelt to get the money and her reticule, he turned steely dark eyes on Mrs. Clark. "I've been hearin' some lies you've been spreadin' about my girl, and I'm warnin' you if they don't stop, I'll be standin' on your porch again."

"Don't you dare threaten me," she shouted.

"Stop the tale bearing!" Pa said and turned his back on her.

"Don't come here again, or I'll have you arrested," Mrs. Clark shouted, then slammed the door shut.

Ignoring her, Pa asked Nancy, "Do you have all your money?"

"As well as I can remember." Nancy dropped the gold coins into her bag. "Let's get away from here."

As they walked down the street, she said, "I've got enough to buy the dress I want. Is it all right to go ahead and buy it now?"

"As far as I'm concerned. You earned the money. It's yours to spend."

■ ■ ■ ■

Over the next few weeks, the war drew closer to home for Nancy. Enlistment offices were opened in the city. Companies were organized, and she often saw militia drilling in open fields on the island, where a rope corral held hundreds of horses that had been bought for the use of the army.

She continued to stay with the Fosters while Pa was gone, until the loyal forces commandeered the *Wetzel* to haul supplies to the troops quartered at the camp on the island. This placed a financial burden on her father, for although he received a voucher to pay for use of the boat, the banks wouldn't honor the funds because of their lack of money.

Patriotic fervor that had prevailed after local political leaders began a new state movement declined considerably when General Lee moved troops into the counties west of the mountains with the goal of keeping them loyal to the state of Virginia. With the army camp on Wheeling Island, those living near the Ohio River should have felt safe, but Nancy's father hinted at things going on in the army camp he didn't like. She was forbidden to cross to the island. But to add to the security of the western counties, Union troops from Ohio commanded by General McClellan crossed the river and set up camp downriver near Parkersburg.

Near the end of May, Colonel Kelley's regiment in the camp was ordered to leave the city and move east to stop an invasion by Confederate troops. Nancy and her father joined other local residents at the train depot to give the soldiers a joyous send-off. Nancy tried to be cheerful to encourage the soldiers, but she was really downhearted.

"Why such a long face?" her father asked as they turned toward home after the train had departed.

Nancy sensed that the Fosters' nonresistance attitude had influenced her, but she didn't dare admit that to her father.

"The soldiers seemed happy now and confident, as if the country is safe in their hands. But Pa, most of them are just boys. They don't seem to realize that war is more than glory. It's wounds, sickness, death, and hardship. Will they be so happy when they come home again?"

"No. And they won't be boys, either. War soon turns a boy into a man! What worries me is that the Confederates are targeting the B&O now, and the trains can't get through to Baltimore. These boys could be killed before they ever see a battlefield."

"The war is getting closer to us all of the time," Heath told Nancy the next day at noon. "And very few troops remain in the area. The general feeling is that Lee's campaign to take control of the renegade counties and stop the mass meetings and conventions being held to protest secession may be successful."

Looking around to be sure Mrs. Foster wasn't nearby, she asked, "Do you suppose Clay might be with him? Wouldn't it be terrible if the Confederates invade Wheeling and he fights against people he's known all of his life?"

"Yes, it would be terrible, but I've been praying that it won't come to that. Lee's full army may not be coming this way, but he has ordered a small regiment under command of Colonel Porterfield to advance on Wheeling and put a stop to the protests against secession."

"What will we do if this happens?"

"I've been wondering about that. I know a few people across the Ohio, and I think they would take Mother and you in."

Nancy didn't comment, but she wouldn't flee to safety and leave Pa and Heath behind in the danger zone. As the weeks had passed, Nancy had noticed that her thoughts were changing. She didn't think like a girl anymore. A few months ago, she would have been ready to run from the enemy at the first sign of danger. Now she felt like a full-grown woman ready to fight alongside her men.

But less than a week after Kelley's troops left town, his troops met the Confederates commanded by Porterfield in the first land battle of the war near the little town of Philippi. Two days after the battle, Heath made an early morning call to a home near the federal building, heard about the Union success, and hurried home with the news.

"Oh my," Nancy said when she heard the news. "I wonder if Clay was in the fighting."

"Even if he was, you're not to worry. The report is that there were no deaths and only a few wounded. Colonel Kelley was shot through the chest, but he's expected to recover."

"I didn't dream the war would come this close to us."

"Remember, we're involved in a little civil war in the midst of the big conflict. The northern states are determined to bring the South back into the Union. And Virginia is going to fight rather than allow the western counties to join the Federalist cause. Unfortunately, I believe that it will get worse before we see an end to this conflict."

The next afternoon when Nancy left the Foster home, Heath went with her as far as the *Intelligencer* office to pick up a copy of the paper. The usual crowd was gathered around the newspaper building, waiting for the papers to be released. Because her father was always interested in the war news, Nancy tarried to buy a copy of the paper, too. When the newsboys bounded into the streets, the crowd surged forward.

"I'll get a copy for you," Heath said.

Nancy was watching his straight shoulders when she sensed that a man crowded close to her and pushed a piece of paper into her hand. Startled, she turned toward him, but his hat was pulled low over his forehead. She didn't get a look at his face before he disappeared into the crowd. She looked quickly at the scrap of paper and slipped it into her pocket. She started trembling, and her face must have revealed her tension, for when Heath came back with two copies of the paper, he asked, "What is it? Are you ill?"

Nancy shook her head, but Heath took

97

her arm. "I'll walk a little farther with you." He directed her toward the riverfront, and they sat on an empty bench facing the water.

"Can you tell me what happened?"

The strength of his shoulder as it pressed against hers relieved Nancy's tension to a degree. She took the slip of paper from her pocket and told him how she had received it.

"Have you read it?"

She shook her head. "No. I don't think the messenger wanted anyone to know he'd given it to me. And he apparently didn't want to be recognized."

"If you want to keep it a secret, I'll leave you. I just wanted to know what had alarmed you." He stood, and she tugged on his coattail.

"Please stay. I don't want to read it alone."

He sat again. It was a small sheet of paper. There was no address on the outside. Nancy unfolded the paper and scanned it quickly. There wasn't a salutation or signature, but she recognized her brother's writing.

"Clay," she said.

"I sensed as much."

"But how did it get here?"

"I understand that messages pass back and forth between the secessionists and their exiled families. Women are often the messengers."

"A man brought this paper."

"Or a woman dressed in men's clothing. What does he say?"

Glancing around to be sure they were alone, Nancy said, "I'll read it to you:

"We got as far as Harper's Ferry. I've joined the Confederates and was with Colonel Jackson there. Now I'm takin' orders from Colonel Porterfield, and we're guardin' the trains around Grafton. General Lee has got to keep control of the rail-roads. Ain't seen much action."

Voicing the idea that had been in her mind since her brother had left home, she said, "Clay might have fought some of the boys he's known all of his life at Philippi!"

"That's why we call it civil war, my dear. You'd better burn the letter to keep it from falling into the wrong hands."

She nodded. "I'll burn it as soon as I get home. I don't know if I feel better or worse. I've wanted to hear from Clay, but now that I know where he is, I'll be worried about him." She stood. "Thanks for being with me when I read this. I'd like to tell Pa about Clay, but he told me to never mention his name again."

Heath watched her as she slowly walked away with her head down. His soul rebelled at the prospect of war in the same world as Nancy Logan, who had become very important to him. And there were times when he sensed that she considered him as more than a friend and mentor. His mother had often thrown out hints that she would welcome grandchildren, but Heath had never intended to marry. His profession consumed so much of his time that he hadn't felt it was wise to encumber himself with a family. But when had he started wondering if marriage to Nancy would be an encumbrance?

Why had she snagged his interest more than the numerous other women he'd met? Her beauty was more captivating than the average woman's, yet it wasn't physical traits that drew him to her. Rather, he admired her capacity to love more than any woman he knew except his mother. Nancy loved her father and brother without qualification, and he was sure this same type of love would be showered upon her husband and children. She had unlocked his heart and soul, and he shared thoughts and concerns with her that he wouldn't have told anyone else. Perhaps more than anything else that made him realize that she was the only woman in the world for him were those few times when Nancy's gaze had mysteriously met his and his heart had turned over in response. Heath wasn't ready to admit that he loved her, but he sensed that a few more weeks of her company would prove that he was.

As soon as Nancy reached home, she read Clay's message one more time and dropped the paper on the hot coals of the kitchen stove. She mixed enough crust for a rhubarb pie and prepared it for baking. Pa liked warm pie with thick cream on it, and the cream had just been delivered this morning, so it would be fresh. She scrubbed small red potatoes and cooked them with fresh peas and fried a young rooster she'd bought at the market. While she had the oven hot to bake the pie, she stirred up a pan of corn bread and shoved it in the oven.

Her father didn't often compliment Nancy on the food, but after he finished eating, he said, "You're a good cook, girl. More 'n' more, you remind me of your ma. She was a good woman, and you will be, too."

Nancy blushed and stammered, "Thanks, Pa."

While Nancy washed the dishes, her father sat at the table, picked his teeth, and read the newspaper. When she heard him lay aside the paper, Nancy's hands hovered over the water. Without turning, she said, "Clay is all right. He's in Grafton under command of Colonel Porterfield."

Nancy held her breath, wondering how her father would react. He seldom lost his temper with her, but perhaps she'd pushed him too far this time. After all, he'd told her never to mention Clay's name again. Silence filled the room, and the clock ticked off the minutes. When he didn't speak, Nancy continued washing the dishes and drying them. Ten minutes or more must have passed before she poured the dishwater down the drain and hung up the dish towel.

"How did you find out?" Pa asked, and Nancy drew a deep breath.

"You're better off not to know."

He got up from the table. "Thanks," he said quietly, then walked to the door and went downstairs.

Nancy buried her face in her hands, and hot tears rolled down her cheeks.

"Thank You, God," she whispered. "He hasn't cast his son aside. He still loves him. But God, have mercy on us."

EIGHT

Nancy counted her money again and with resolve walked into a store on Main Street. How she wished Stella were here to advise her! Most of the dresses were made to order, but the proprietor always had a few gowns made ahead. Nancy hoped she had enough money to buy what she wanted. Today was the first of July, and there was no time to have a dress made especially for her.

Now that the country was at war and she had seen firsthand how much it cost to wage war, Nancy wondered if she wasn't being selfish to spend her money on clothes. But a big Independence Day celebration was planned on the island, and since she had worked so hard and saved to have a new dress, she decided she might as well go ahead and buy one.

Clutching her reticule tightly, Nancy approached Pearl Martin, the saleswoman.

She would choose the dress first and see how much money she had left for accessories.

"I want to buy a readymade dress."

Pearl measured Nancy's height, around her waist, across her shoulders. "We only have two that will fit you," she said apologetically. "Our supply is very low. I used to order my material from Richmond, and that isn't possible anymore. I order from New York now, and it takes longer for shipments to arrive. I have this dark green silk."

Nancy shook her head. "I don't think so. I wanted something in a light color."

The second dress couldn't have pleased her more if she'd placed an order for it.

She tried on the white silk petticoat and overdress of white crepe, which was trimmed with three rows of pinked ruffles in a light blue. "I'll need to put a tuck or two in the waist if you want this one," Pearl said. "It's a bit long, but if you wear a hoop, the length will be all right."

"I don't have a hoop. Do you have any for sale?"

"Yes, and at a good price, too."

After she paid for the dress and hoop, Nancy had to choose between a new pair of shoes and a hat. The dress was long enough to conceal her old shoes, so she used the rest of her money to buy a leghorn bonnet with a wide white ribbon and a bunch of violets on the left side. Pearl made a few tucks in the waist of the dress and buttoned the dress up the back. As Nancy tied the bonnet in place, Pearl turned her to face the wide, floor-length mirror. Nancy could hardly believe it was her image looking back at her.

"I'm sure you'll enjoy these clothes. They've turned you from a girl into a grown-up lady," Pearl said. Her words encouraged Nancy, for sometimes she believed that Heath still thought of her as a child.

The saleswoman wrapped Nancy's purchases in white paper and smiled as she opened the door for her. Nancy hurried toward home. She couldn't wait for Heath to see her in such finery. But her steps slowed when Nancy remembered that the Quakers were plain people. Considering the simple, unadorned dresses that Mrs. Foster wore, Nancy wondered if she had chosen the right garments to snag Heath's attention. But she put these worries aside and counted the minutes until the great day.

The celebration wasn't scheduled until three o'clock, but Nancy and her father left the house soon after noon because they wanted to find a shady place to sit. They crossed a small swinging bridge to the island and walked to the army camp, where the festivities were to take place. When she'd modeled her new garments for her father, he'd looked her over carefully and shrugged his shoulders. "If you're happy to be dressed that way, it's okay with me."

Considering his lack of praise, she wasn't as happy with her appearance as she'd expected to be.

Although she'd looked forward to this occasion for months, she felt ill at ease. When she saw Colonel Kelley, who was still recuperating from his wounds, and the other soldiers sitting in places of honor on the platform, Nancy again questioned if it was unpatriotic for her to spend all of her money on clothes she didn't need. She was tempted to go back home and change, but a lot of people had already seen her. Besides, the ceremony was ready to start, and she didn't want to miss any of the speeches.

Nancy sat on a blanket with several girls who attended her church. Her father joined a group of men standing near the platform. Most everyone had a flag pinned on his or her clothing.

After speeches by the town's dignitaries

and a few words from Colonel Kelley, a bugler played a favorite hymn. The words found lodging in Nancy's heart, and as she listened to the gentle strains of the instrument, she prayed the words in her heart as her fondest hope for her country:

O God, our help in ages past,
Our hope for years to come,
Our shelter from the stormy blast,
And our eternal home.

The celebration ended when the national flag was hoisted to the top of the pole. Church bells started ringing in the city. Rockets soared high above the assemblage. Drums sounded. Men and boys shot rifles into the air. The crowd applauded and cheered heartily. Nancy's heart swelled with love and pride of her country, and it was difficult to believe that the nation could be divided.

Nancy had looked around several times to see if Heath had come to the celebration, but she hadn't seen him. So her dream of playing the elegant lady in his presence had backfired. *Pride goeth before destruction,* she silently chided herself as she tried to get up off the ground in her billowing skirts.

Giggling, one of her friends pulled on her

right hand while Nancy held her skirts in place. In an attempt to hide her embarrassment, Nancy smiled broadly. She walked across the field toward her father and came face-to-face with Heath, who stared at her as if he was seeing her for the first time.

"You're beautiful," he murmured huskily.

"Oh! I didn't know you were here."

"I had a sick patient here on the island. I was late, so I stayed in the background rather than interrupt the program. May I walk you home?"

"I guess that will be all right. I'll tell Pa."

Her father had gone onstage to shake hands with Colonel Kelley, but when he turned toward her, she pointed to Heath and waved. Pa interpreted her message and agreed by nodding.

Many people were leaving the army camp, so they weren't alone, but Heath said quietly, "Perhaps I spoke out of turn, but I've never seen you in such elegant garments. They become you."

"Thank you. I've wanted a dress like this since I saw the pretty clothes Stella wore. Pa didn't object, but he said I'd have to earn the money to buy a new dress. That's why I went to work for Tabitha Clark. But I haven't enjoyed wearing them today. When our country is at war, I shouldn't have spent so much money on fripperies."

"I'm sorry you feel that way. The dress and hat are perfect for you."

"That makes me feel better."

They crossed the small bridge single file. Heath's horse was tied to a post along the wharf, but it was only a short distance to the Logan home. He walked with her, chatting about the celebration.

Since the army had commandeered the *Wetzel,* Nancy's father was home at night, and Heath had missed his talks with Nancy.

As if she'd read his thoughts, Nancy said, "Pa has had some good news. The army has released his boat so he can start making his usual runs. He'll be busy for several weeks delivering the shipments that have backed up in the warehouses."

"Does that mean you'll be staying at our home while he's gone?"

"I don't know. After the Union victory at Philippi, it seems like everything has calmed down, so he may tell me to stay at home."

"Mother and I like your company."

"Thanks."

"Have you heard anything more from your brother?"

"No, and it worries me. I'd like to know that he's all right. Do you think the war will end soon?"

Heath frowned and threaded his hair with his long, slender fingers. "I can't say this to anyone else without being taken for a traitor, but I don't believe there will be a speedy resolution of this conflict. Some of our country's best generals have joined the Confederacy, and they'll be fighting a defensive war."

"I don't know what that means."

"All the South wants is to be left alone. And I believe they have the manpower to keep the Federal armies out of their states. It's easier to defend what they have than for the Northern armies to invade a hostile territory. The fighting could drag on for years."

They had reached Nancy's home and paused at the foot of the steps. "Pa will be home soon if you want to wait."

He shook his head. "I have some work to do, but I've enjoyed our walk."

He lifted her hand, kissed her palm gently, turned abruptly, and left. He had noted surprise and confusion on Nancy's face, and he wondered if she had resented his caress.

Although the citizens of Wheeling had come together to celebrate Independence Day, much unrest still filled the city. The local authorities attempted to keep a tight rein on crime, but Pa worried about Nancy's safety. "Because your brother joined the Confederate Army, some people are suspicious of us. I don't like for you to be alone, even in the daytime. The attitude of people in this town changes according to who's winning the war, and right now, the Confederates seem to be."

"I heard Dr. Foster say that people are afraid the Confederacy will be victorious in its attempt to establish a separate country, and if it is, Virginia will invade its rebellious northwestern counties and force us to stay with the mother state."

"And it could happen. I'm a loyal Union man, but everybody's got a right to live accordin' to the dictates of his own conscience. Even if I don't agree with a man, I ain't gonna burn down his house or deny him his freedom. If I was a bettin' man, I'd wager that before the year is out, secessionists in this town will be arrested. And when Doc Foster keeps on treatin' Confederate sympathizers the same as he doctors anybody else, he'll probably end up in jail, too. That just ain't right."

Her father's prediction worried Nancy, but the days passed, and Heath wasn't arrested. Never knowing when he might be put in jail, Nancy cherished every moment she was with him. They didn't have many opportunities to be alone, but during those few times, a delicate thread of magnetism formed between them. He sometimes held her hand, once he had kissed her on the forehead, and when he knew she was worrying about Clay, he gathered her gently into his arms, holding her until the bad moment passed. A tangible bond brought them together, and she often wondered what the future held for them.

As the heat of summer invaded Wheeling, the Fosters spent more time on their front porch. While Mrs. Foster and Nancy prepared sewing kits for soldiers, Heath pored over the latest edition of the *Intelligencer*. He also subscribed to *Harper's Weekly,* and the week after Wheeling's Independence Day celebration, he said, "Wheeling made headlines in the *Weekly*."

Willing to rest her eyes for a moment, Nancy laid aside her sewing and looked up. "Good or bad news?"

Grinning, Heath said, "That depends on the reader, I suppose. This is the July 6 issue. They have an illustration of the third floor of the district federal courtroom of Wheeling's U.S. Custom House."

He passed the newspaper to Nancy as he continued to explain. "In an earlier issue,

Harper's highlighted the May meeting when delegates met in Wheeling and called for a new state of Virginia — one loyal to the Union. This article mentions the Second Wheeling Convention, convened after a majority of Virginians voted for secession."

Nancy's eyebrows puckered thoughtfully. "I understood that the delegates want a new state."

"They do, and the Congress of the United States is apparently willing to approve a separate state, but the Constitution provides that a state can't be formed within a state unless the mother state approves. The Richmond legislature would never give their consent, so our lawmakers intend to create a reorganized Virginia government, which *will* agree to form a separate state."

"Sounds like that might not be legal," Nancy said.

Heath laughed, for he liked the keenness of Nancy's mind. "You've hit the nail on the head! Some of our delegates agree with you. That's the subject of the article — you can read it."

Nancy read a few paragraphs, then turned to Heath, perplexity wrinkling her forehead.

"It would feel strange to live in the same city but be a part of a new state. What would the state's name be?"

"Several have been suggested. Let me name some of them, and you can decide which you like best." Listing them on his fingers, he said, "Allegheny. Augusta. Kanawha. New Virginia. West Virginia."

"I was born in Wheeling, and I've always been a Virginian. I think I'd choose a name that had Virginia in it. West Virginia sounds good to me. Will this happen right away?"

"It will probably take a year or so before all the political decisions are made. And a lot can happen before then."

"But if the Confederacy takes control of the western counties again, we would stay a part of Virginia."

"Yes, and we would be fighting a civil war in our own state. A lot of blood will be shed if that were to happen, and the very thought distresses me."

In less than a month, Nancy realized that Heath's prediction about the length of the war was probably true. The Confederates' stunning victory at the Battle of Bull Run brought the grim reality of war home to Wheeling families, when several of their sons were killed and sent home in wooden coffins. Fearing the reaction if the Confederates won the war, some of Nancy's neighbors moved into Ohio. And when she had no further word from Clay, Nancy worried that he might have fallen in battle and that she would never know.

Perhaps concerned about the same thing, her father became morose and bitter. And his worries increased when the packet business declined after factories closed because their workers were drafted into the army. The only peace Nancy found was in the Foster home, and she was there often after her father was hired by the army to use the *Wetzel* to haul supplies. He was away from home several nights each week, but while the country seemed on its way to being torn apart, the emotional relationship between Nancy and Heath continued to grow.

NINE

One November evening as Heath and Nancy walked slowly along the street in front of the U.S. Custom House, she said, "Even though it's been talked about for months, it's still hard for me to believe that people in that building are making plans for the counties west of the Allegheny Mountains to form a new state that would be loyal to the Union."

"It is rather amazing," Heath agreed. "But it isn't as easy as it sounds. The formation of a new state may not be constitutional."

"Yes, I remember we talked about that several weeks ago."

" 'No new State shall be formed or erected within the jurisdiction of any other state; nor any state be formed by the junction of two or more States, or parts of states, without the consent of the legislatures of the states concerned as well as of the Congress.' "

Nancy's mouth dropped open, and she stared wide-eyed at him. "Imagine! Being able to quote part of the federal constitution from memory!"

With an apologetic smile, Heath said, "I wasn't trying to flaunt my knowledge. But I've been studying that section for a week or two — trying to figure out if the steps we're taking to organize a new state are legal."

"But you would favor such a move?"

Heath continued to talk as they moved toward the Logan home. "Yes, I think it's the only logical step our delegates can take. The two sections of the state have very little in common. Not only are we separated from the Tidewater counties by rugged mountain terrain, but there are economic, political, social, and cultural differences, as well."

They wandered on toward the river and sat side by side on a bench. Nancy buttoned her coat, for although winter was late in coming this year, the nights were cool.

With a smile, he asked, "Are you sure I'm not boring you with all of this?"

"Oh no," Nancy hastened to assure him. "It's important for me to know why we want to form a new state. Clay was so convinced that the government in Richmond was right in its decision to secede that he was willing to give up his family and home to fight for what he believed in. When I ask Pa about the political situation, he starts ranting that Virginia shouldn't have seceded, but he never says why. Tell me all you can."

"I'll make it brief. Because the mountains prevented easy trading with the eastern seaboard, Virginians in the west found markets for their goods in Ohio and Pennsylvania, while the eastern section shipped to the northern and southern states."

"I remember studying in school that the people are different, too," Nancy added. "The mountaineers, mostly Scotch-Irish and German, are more democratic and less aristocratic than the residents along the seaboard who can trace their ancestral roots to England."

"That's true. I didn't know much about the Appalachian region until I moved to Wheeling, but I've learned that the people who live here are a breed apart from those along the seaboard. Both areas were settled by Europeans, but from varied backgrounds."

A steamboat traveled past, going downstream, and the captain blew the whistle in greeting. The sound had been familiar to Nancy all of her life, and she waved to him, wishing she could go back to those carefree times of her childhood. She acknowledged sadly that because of this conflict waging around them, the old ways were gone forever. But the fact that she was accepting these changes and changing with them indicated that she was leaving her childhood behind.

"Perhaps slavery is the greatest difference in the sections now," Heath continued. "The Tidewater counties depend on slave labor for their livelihood. In comparison, there are very few slaves in the Trans-Allegheny regions. The rugged country has developed into small farms, making slave labor impractical."

"But slavery doesn't cause any trouble in Wheeling."

"That's because there are fewer than fifty slaves in the town. Most of them are household servants and treated well. And if they should be mistreated, it's easy to cross the Ohio River and be in free territory." Heath stood. "It will be dark soon. I'll walk you home."

As autumn passed into winter, Pa's temperament rose and fell depending on how much work he had to do. He was cranky through most of November. His usual runs to Parkersburg and his trips for the army were disrupted by a lack of rain that kept the channels closed to river traffic. Nancy was down in the dumps, too, for she hadn't had much opportunity to see Heath. For a couple of weeks he was busy with a bout of sore throats and lung inflammation in Wheeling and the countryside, and with her father at home, it hadn't been necessary for her to spend nights with the Fosters.

Nancy realized that she was becoming too serious about Heath. Except for a few times, he hadn't given any indication that he had any more consideration for her than any other woman. But a week of hard rains in early winter raised the river level, and the week after Thanksgiving Nancy's father made a run to Parkersburg. Upon his return, he stopped to pick up Nancy at the Foster residence. Heath happened to be home, and Pa asked to see him.

"Come in, Mr. Logan," Heath said when he came to the door.

"No, thankee. I've got to do some repair on the *Wetzel*'s engine before I head back downstream." Nancy came to the door with her satchel, and Heath opened the door for her and followed her out on the porch.

"Nancy mentioned that you want to talk to somebody who practices herbal medicine."

"Yes," Heath said eagerly. "I've long been interested in finding new medicines. Because of the restrictions of war, my plans to talk to herbalists living in the Appalachian region have been thwarted. I can't very well go into the mountains when there's a civil war going on."

"You don't have to go to the mountains," Pa said, looking pleased about the information he had to share. "There's a woman as close as Parkersburg, who's supposed to be an expert on herbs. Her home is in the mountains south of the Kanawha River, but there's so much fighting going on there that she moved to Parkersburg to live with her daughter. If you've a mind to, you can ride with me on the *Wetzel* free of charge."

"I certainly want to take the opportunity to talk to the woman," Heath said eagerly. "Most of my patients with colds and other ailments are better now, so I can probably leave for a few days. When will your next trip be?"

"Not until I get the engine fixed on the *Wetzel,* which I hope ain't more'n five or six days, for I've got a lot of freight to haul. I'll send word by Nancy."

Heath glanced at his mother, who had come to the door and heard. "I don't know of any reason I shouldn't go. Do you?"

"I've been taking turns looking after our sick neighbor, but if both of you are gone, I'll stay home to look after Nancy."

"Don't need to change your plans, ma'am," Pa said. "Nancy can ride along with us on the boat. There's a little cabin where she can sleep. She goes with me sometimes when I'm not crowded."

Nancy couldn't think of anything she would enjoy more than a trip on the steamboat with Heath. And the opportunity had been dumped into her lap without any effort on her part. Nancy felt Heath's eyes on her, but she didn't look at him. Was it possible that her father was matchmaking?

When the *Wetzel* weighed anchor five days later, Nancy and Heath, shoulders touching, stood at the bow looking at the riverbank where leafless deciduous trees gave a gaunt appearance to the landscape. Nancy scanned the hills where a few evergreens added some color to the countryside. Sunrays highlighted the rugged bluffs behind the city.

Nancy shivered when a cold wind swept around them. "The hills are pretty even after the leaves fall."

"During the first year after I moved here, I wondered if I would ever get used to the hills. I'd always lived in Philadelphia, and I didn't know much about the rest of the country. I've learned to love this area, though, and I wouldn't be happy to live in the East again."

"I'm happy to hear that," Nancy said. "I would miss you and your mother if you left Wheeling."

Heath didn't answer, and he stared moodily at the water. When he left Philadelphia, he had thought his future was well defined. Knowing the demanding hours of a physician right from the beginning, he had decided that a medical practice and family life didn't mix. He had chosen medical research and the practice of medicine as his priorities.

He glanced at Nancy, half annoyed because meeting her had disrupted his plans. When he had his life ordered, why had he become so enamored with this young woman, ten years younger than he, which in itself presented a problem? Although many men married women much younger than they were, from a doctor's standpoint, he didn't approve of it. He'd seen too many young widows left with a passel of children to raise by themselves. And he had no idea what she thought of him. How could she stand there so calm and serene as if this were an ordinary day, when he hadn't been able to sleep the night before because he'd been contemplating the few days they would have together?

He looked up toward Wendell Logan in the pilothouse as he steered the *Wetzel* into the deepest channel of the Ohio. In a few succinct words, Wendell had once made it known what he thought of Quakers. So considering the differences in age and spiritual beliefs that stood between Nancy and him, why couldn't he put her out of his mind?

But knowing that two or three days with Nancy would be an opportunity he might not have again, Heath put his somber assumptions aside. As Wendell unerringly steered the *Wetzel* toward Parkersburg, Heath settled down to enjoy the trip. His problems could be resolved after they returned to Wheeling.

Because of a late start from Wheeling, which necessitated an overnight stop, it was noon of the second day before the *Wetzel* arrived in Parkersburg. After giving his crew orders about unloading the cargo, Wendell walked with Heath and Nancy up the riverbank toward the town of Parkersburg. Nancy looked with interest at the general stores and a few restaurants, not unlike the buildings they had at home. Wendell stopped in front of a two-story brick building with HOTEL painted in large gold letters across the front.

"The owner of this hotel is the one who told me about the herb woman. We can eat in the hotel restaurant, and I'll see if I can find out where she lives."

The hotel was near the waterfront, and compared to the elegance of the McClure House in Wheeling, Nancy considered it to be a little shabby. Heath held the door for her, and Nancy stepped inside. Her eyes were immediately drawn to a young woman standing in the lobby. The shock of discovery stopped Nancy in her tracks, and she took a quick breath of utter astonishment.

"Stella?" she murmured, and at her voice, the young woman looked her way. It *was* Stella.

Nancy ran toward her friend. "Why, Stella! I supposed you would be in Alabama by now. What are you doing here?"

Tears formed in Stella's eyes, and she threw her arms around Nancy. "Because we don't have any other place to go," she said bitterly. "You'll never believe all the things that have happened to us."

Nancy felt a hand on her shoulder.

"I'm here," Heath said, and Nancy's heart lifted, as she realized that he would know what to do and say in this situation. Her father was talking to the hotel clerk and apparently hadn't noticed Stella's presence.

"We're going to eat dinner here, Stella," Heath said. "Where's your family? Could all of you join us?"

Nancy gave him a grateful look. His calm presence helped to steady her erratic pulse, and she prayed that she could be of some help to her friend. Tears cascaded down Stella's face, and Nancy put an arm around her. Nancy and Heath exchanged concerned glances over Stella's shaking shoulders.

"Has something happened to your parents?" Nancy asked.

Stella shook her head. "No, they're safe. But we've had a horrible time — just horrible!"

"Let's sit over here on this divan," Heath said. "You can tell us about it."

Nancy turned Stella toward a quiet area near the stairway. When they sat down, Nancy pulled a handkerchief from her reticule and wiped the tears from Stella's face as she continued to hold her hand firmly.

"Tell us what has happened," Nancy insisted.

Pa joined them, surprise on his face. Stella seemed to take courage from his presence, for she had once admitted that she felt more comfortable around Nancy's pa than she did her own father.

"We left Parkersburg a week after you brought us here, Mr. Logan. Everything went well enough until we got to Cincinnati and learned that Federal troops had closed the river to all southbound traffic. They wouldn't let any boats pass Cincinnati unless they agreed to stay on the northern Ohio. And even the northbound traffic was at a standstill for weeks."

Stella had calmed considerably by now. She glanced from one to the other of the three sympathetic faces before her. "You can't imagine how good it is to see you."

"Why did you wait so long to come back?" Heath asked.

"Papa was determined to go to Alabama. He tried to find overland passage, but Kentucky is a battleground, too, just like Virginia. It wouldn't have been safe, even if we could have found someone to take us. Train travel into the Confederacy has stopped." She started crying again but continued in a quavering voice. "Just because we talked like Southerners and wanted to go to Alabama, people treated us like spies. We waited around, thinking that the Confederate Army might open the river, but that didn't happen. We spent all the money Papa had, and he sold Mama's jewelry to get enough money to pay our passage back to Wheeling."

Heath and Nancy exchanged troubled glances. The way distrust was accelerating against secessionists in Wheeling, Nancy doubted that the Danford family would receive any better treatment there.

"Will you take us with you when you go home?" Stella asked Pa.

"I'm not sure I can take you this trip. We'll have to tie up at night, and Nancy is sleeping in the cabin."

"That's okay, Pa. I'll share the room with Stella and her mother. Or I can sleep in the pilothouse with you."

"Let me go and bring Papa to talk to you," Stella pleaded. "He's awful worried about Mama. She cries all the time and covers her face when we're out in public — she says all she wants to do is go inside her house and never see anyone again."

"I'll tuck you in somewhere," Pa agreed.

Giving him a grateful smile, Stella hurried up the stairway.

"Ain't that a shame!" Pa said. "Why didn't the hotheads who started this war look

128

ahead and see what their flying off the handle would cause? We had a good country, so why did they have to tear it apart and ruin the lives of good people like the Danfords?"

"And I didn't have the heart to tell Stella that their home has been confiscated by the army," Nancy said. Hearing footsteps on the stairs, she turned around.

She couldn't believe that the stooped, defeated man walking toward them was Sinclair Danford. She had always stood in awe of Stella's father, who wore only the best, tailor-made garments and whose bearing proclaimed that he was proud of being a self-made man. Stella loved her father deeply, but Nancy had always considered him a dominating man, whose attitude had probably turned Stella's mother into the weak-willed woman she was.

Mr. Danford shook hands with Heath and her father and nodded in Nancy's direction. His gray eyes were dismal. His usually trim beard was scruffy, and his hair didn't look as if it had been combed for days. He straightened his shoulders, but that gesture did little to disguise his defeated attitude.

Addressing Wendell, he said, "My daughter says you will take us back to Wheeling."

"Yes. It will be crowded for your womenfolk, but I'll make them as comfortable as possible."

"We came here from Cincinnati on a boat pushing two barges loaded with cattle. Your accommodations can't be any worse than that. When are you leaving?"

"Probably day after tomorrow. Doc Foster has some business to take care of here in Parkersburg, and I'll be loading cargo tomorrow. I'll let you know."

Mr. Danford turned away, and Heath invited, "Will you and your family have dinner with us as my guests?"

Danford rejected the invitation with a cold smile. "We don't have to take charity yet. Besides, my wife is indisposed. I'll send Stella down if she wants to share your meal."

Ten

Mattie Sawyers was like no one Nancy had ever seen. After a mile's walk outside the city limits, they located the mountain woman at her daughter's home. The wizened, stooped woman was about five feet tall. Her frowsy gray hair framed a face as wrinkled as a monkey's, but the hooded black eyes that peered from under bushy gray brows gleamed with an inner fire of mystery and intelligence.

"So ye want to learn my secrets, do ye?" she said with a cackle when Heath sat near her on the porch of the modest frame cottage.

"I'm a doctor, Mrs. Sawyers, and I'm interested in learning anything and everything that will bring healing to the sick and wounded. I'm convinced that herbal remedies are superior to some of the patent medicines I can buy."

She nodded her head emphatically.

"You're right about that. I'll gladly tell you what I know, for there ain't many folks want to learn the old ways," she said. "My young'uns would druther buy a bottle of Dr. Flint's Quaker Bitters from peddlers than take a dose of my wild ginger tea that will fix them up after a few teaspoonfuls."

"My mother and I grow a small garden of herbs, and I sometimes use those in treating my patients, but with your experience, you must know more about native plants than I do. I'll be obliged if you will share that knowledge with me."

"I will, sonny. I ain't gonna live much longer, and it will do my heart good to know that a fine young man like you will carry on my healin' know-how."

Nancy sat in the background during the next two hours, content to listen as Mrs. Sawyers, in her quaint mountaineer voice, explained the secret of nature's healing to Heath. She talked slowly, and he quickly recorded what she told him.

Nancy recognized that some of the remedies were made from familiar plants. She was surprised to learn that salves could be made by boiling chickweed, plantain, water lily roots, and sour dock. Tansy was used for sick headache, chamomile was good for a tonic, dandelion and fennel for colic, marigold blossoms would cure colds, and mashed catnip leaves could relieve the itching of hives. Taken altogether, Nancy considered it a profitable visit for Heath, and after they left the woman's home, he agreed that the knowledge he'd gained from Mrs. Sawyer would be helpful in his research.

"I learned more from her in a few hours than from many of the classes I took in medical school. I'll have to study all of this information and decide how I can adapt it to treating my patients. I have a book that lists different plants in the United States, some of them growing in other climates. Hopefully, when this war stops, I can travel to look for them. In the meantime, I'll search for the plants growing in the Wheeling area. Will you help me look for these herbs?"

"Yes, I like to wander around in the woods and fields. I recognized some of the plants she named."

"I wouldn't prescribe any of these herbal treatments to my patients until I've done a great deal of research on them and discussed them with my learned colleagues, but I've always been interested in learning more about herbal medicines. There's so much about curing the human body that we don't know." He continued to discuss what he'd heard from Mrs. Sawyers, and although Nancy was interested in what they'd learned and hesitated to interrupt him, she was troubled about Stella and her family. Heath paused in thought about the time the houses of Parkersburg came into view, and Nancy asked, "Should we tell Mr. Danford that his home has been confiscated by the army to store supplies for the army camp on the island?"

Sighing, Heath answered, "He needs to know before we get to Wheeling. I'm hoping your father will tell him."

"Wonder what they'll do — where will they live?"

"He owns a few cottages down near his factory. They may have to move into one of them. Perhaps he'll start the factory again, although he may not have enough raw materials to resume operation, for he depended on cotton from the South to make his products. Now that the Ohio and Mississippi river valleys have become battlegrounds, there won't be much raw cotton available in the North."

"Nobody considered all of those things when the war started, did they?"

"People in general didn't think at all — only irrational people would want a war."

Nancy didn't comment, and she wouldn't

tell her father what Heath had said, for they seemed to be getting along all right now. She hadn't heard Pa mention Heath's Quaker heresy for several weeks, and she didn't want to remind him of Heath's views on the war.

Heath took a room in the hotel overnight, but he had supper with Wendell and Nancy before they went to the *Wetzel.* Before they parted from Heath, Nancy said, "Pa, are you going to tell Mr. Danford before we get to Wheeling that they don't have a home?"

He threw up his hands. "Not me! They ought to know, all right, but I don't speak Danford's language. Doc, you can talk to him."

With a resigned shrug of his shoulders, Heath said, "I suppose there's nothing else to do. I hate to hit a man when he's down, but he must be told."

The return trip to Wheeling held none of the serenity and pleasure for Nancy that she'd enjoyed with Heath as they had traveled to Parkersburg. Mrs. Danford spent all of her time in the small room that Nancy had occupied, and Stella stayed with her. Their spirits were so low the first day that Nancy was depressed, too, and she stayed several hours on deck with Heath. It seemed that every time she glanced toward the pilothouse, her father was watching them. When darkness approached and the boat docked for the night, she spread some blankets in the pilothouse where her father slept.

The air was cold, but Nancy and Pa weren't sleepy, so they sat alone on the hurricane deck as darkness fell around them. Nancy's thoughts lingered on the Danfords' problems, and she wished she could do more to help Stella. Her father was less talkative than usual, and Nancy wondered what was on his mind. When he spoke, she was sorry to learn what he was thinking about.

"Daughter, I'm worried about you seeing so much of Doc Foster. I wish I hadn't brought you along on this trip. He's got his good points, but I can't trust no man who ain't willin' to fight for his country. Besides, he's gonna end up in prison for helping the enemy. You're gonna have to stay away from him."

"But Pa," Nancy protested. Pa raised a hand to silence her.

"I ain't finished. I won't keep you from going to work for Mrs. Foster in the daytime and helpin' with her work for the soldiers, but you can't stay at night. And I don't want him drivin' or walkin' you home like he's been doin'. I've been kinda lax in that because of the differences in your ages, but it appears to me that you're growing up mighty fast lately. And if the matter should happen to come up, I want you to know how I stand on any courtship between you and Doc Foster."

Nancy dropped her head and bit her lips to stop the quivering. So much for her wondering if her father was matchmaking between Heath and her!

He stood up and headed toward the pilothouse. "It's time to go to sleep," he said, and although Nancy wanted to beg him to change his mind, she knew it would be useless. She went inside and lay down on the pallet she'd prepared earlier. Her father wrapped a blanket around his shoulders and lay near the door.

After Nancy heard his even breathing and his usual cacophony of snoring, she gave way to the sobs she'd been stifling since her father's ultimatum. She knew now that she loved Heath, and to be deprived of his company would be heartbreaking.

Why did she have to lose everybody she loved? She'd lost her mother when she was only a girl. Clay was gone, and she wondered if she would ever see him again. Now she was forbidden to have anything to do with Heath, who had brought more pleasure into her life than anyone she had ever known. But she would have to obey her father, or he would go to Heath and tell him that he didn't want his daughter keeping company with a coward.

Nancy cried until her eyes burned and her nasal passages were congested. She sat up and gasped for breath. She leaned against the wall and waited until morning. If she could only pray, it would have made the hours pass, but there seemed to be a wall between her and God.

Her father had said she could continue working for Mrs. Foster, but Nancy knew she couldn't. Pa didn't realize that Heath was in and out of the house all day long, so she couldn't obey her father if she still worked there. She faced a dreary existence, for not only was she losing Heath, but she was also giving up the friendship of Mrs. Foster, whom she regarded almost as a mother.

When daylight came and Pa stirred, Nancy threw the blanket aside, stood, and walked outside and gulped the fresh morning air. Pa walked by, and apparently unconcerned over the emotional blow he'd tossed into her life, he said, "I'm gonna get some breakfast. We'll be under way in no time and home by midafternoon."

Nancy didn't answer, trying to think of some way she could avoid Heath until they reached Wheeling. She stayed on the upper deck until the *Wetzel* pushed away from the bank and accessed the deeper waters of the river. She didn't know where Heath had spent the night, but keeping an eye out for him, she scuttled down a rear stairway that led to the galley to get some breakfast for Stella and her mother. Her own stomach was queasy, and she didn't feel like eating.

"Hi, Tom," she said quietly, relieved to see that the cook was alone.

The cook's face spread into a toothy smile. "Hi, lil' Nancy."

Tom, an aging, brawny man, had worked on the *Wetzel* several years, and he still considered her a child. He was a jack-of-all-trades, but he always did the cooking.

"You hungry?"

"No, but I'd like some food for Mrs. Danford and Stella."

He wagged his shaggy white head. "Poor folks. Too bad about them. My boy worked for Mr. Danford — he treated his workers right."

Tom lifted a tray from the cupboard. "I'll

put some batter cakes, honey, and sausage on here — enough for all three of you." He peered keenly at Nancy. "You look a little out of curl, this mawnin'. What's wrong?"

"I'm all right. Do you have any tea?"

He scratched his head. " 'Fraid not, missy. We don't carry womenfolk very much. All I've got is coffee."

She had tasted Tom's coffee once, and she knew Mrs. Danford would turn up her nose at the strong brew. "I'd better take a jar of water, then."

Tom poured water into a jar, capped it, and put it on the tray.

"Careful!" he admonished when Nancy lifted the tray with trembling hands. "Maybe I'd better carry it for you."

"No, I'll manage. Thanks, Tom. I'll bring the tray back."

Heath was standing at the bow of the *Wetzel* when Nancy rounded the corner. He moved eagerly toward her, but she shook her head at him and dodged into the small stateroom, where she intended to stay until the steamboat reached Wheeling. The room was stuffy, and Mrs. Danford's sighs nearly drove her to distraction, but that was better than facing Heath. Yet didn't he deserve an explanation? After a few hours, she came to a decision.

"Stella," she said, "I want to write a note, and I don't feel very well. Will you go to Pa's office and see if you can find a sheet of paper and a pencil? I'll stay with your mother."

Stella had been sitting on the floor and leaning against the cot where her mother lay, but she jumped up eagerly.

"Yes, I'd be glad to." With a worried look at her mother, she whispered, "Thank you for asking — I don't think I could have endured another moment in this room. I need a breath of fresh air."

"Take your time. It will be awhile before we reach Wheeling."

Heath chose a seat where he could watch the door to the cabin. When Nancy didn't show up, he impatiently decided that if she didn't come out soon, he would knock on the door and ask about her. He stood quickly when he saw a woman come out of the cabin, but frowned in disappointment when he recognized Stella.

The bright sun must have blinded her momentarily, for she stopped, leaned against the rail, and shaded her eyes. Heath hurried toward her and lifted his hat.

"And how is your mother, Stella?" She jumped slightly, and he apologized for startling her. "I'm willing to help if she needs medical treatment."

Stella shook her head, and he saw tears glistening in her eyes. "Thank you, but she isn't physically ill. Her whole world has been destroyed, and her heart is broken. You don't have a pill for that kind of sickness, do you?"

"Unfortunately, no."

She turned away, and he said slowly, "Is Miss Logan still in the cabin with you?"

"Yes, and she must have realized that I was almost near the breaking point, too, for she asked me to run an errand for her while she stayed with Mama."

"Then she isn't sick?"

"I don't know. She looks sad and awful peaked. But that room is so stuffy, it's no wonder she looks sickly. Mama won't let us keep the door open. Nice to talk to you, Dr. Foster, but I have to go."

"When you go back, will you tell Miss Logan that I'd like to see her?"

Stella nodded her head and turned toward the stern of the steamboat.

Heath sensed that something was wrong, for he thought that Wendell had avoided him this morning, too. He looked speculatively at the pilothouse where Nancy's father stood, both hands on the wheel, eyes intensely focused on the river in front of him. What could have happened in such a short time to make the Logans evade him?

Too restless to sit down, Heath paced the main deck, keeping his eyes on the cabin door. The *Wetzel*'s whistle sounded loudly, indicating that it would soon be docking, and when the boat rounded a small curve in the Ohio, he caught sight of the taller buildings in Wheeling. Just as he had given up hope of seeing Nancy, he saw Stella approaching. He turned eagerly toward her. She walked close to him and slipped a piece of paper in his hand before she hurried away. Amazed, Heath stared at the note. He unfolded the wrinkled paper.

Heath, please forgive me for avoiding you today. It would be too embarrassing to tell you why I had to do this. I won't come out of the cabin until you leave the boat. Tell your mother that I can't work for her. Try to understand. Don't hate me.

Heath read the message again, trying to make sense of it. He knew from her brief message that the decision had been made by Wendell Logan rather than Nancy. Why? When the war started, Wendell had been very curt with Heath about his political views, but as the war effort had intensified, he believed that Wendell had changed his mind. Sentiment in Wheeling, however, was becoming more biased against secessionists and pacifists, and it wasn't wise for anyone to befriend them.

He was the first one to walk down the gangplank when the boat docked, and he hurried toward his home without a backward glance. In that moment when Heath knew he had lost Nancy, he realized that he loved her. He had tried to tell himself that he didn't want a family to interfere with his plans to devote his life to medical research. He had argued with himself that he was ten years older than Nancy, although he felt younger when he was with her than at any other time. But now that he knew she was lost to him, none of those arguments were convincing.

My God, he prayed silently, *I can't violate my conscience just to get the woman I love. But now that I've learned the full blessing of love, how can I live without her? If I would swear complete allegiance to the Union cause, it would please Wendell Logan, and he wouldn't be opposed to my courtship of Nancy. But, dear God, how can I choose between my convictions and the woman I love?*

ELEVEN

Spring 1862

Nancy breathed deeply of the mild spring air as she and Stella walked along the banks of the Ohio. Although it was the middle of May, a few dogwood trees were still blooming on the hills, and the trees were almost in full leaf. The goal of statehood for western Virginians loomed ever closer, for just a few days ago the Reorganized Government of Virginia had approved the creation of the new state with forty-eight counties. Believing that eastern Virginia wouldn't lose a large portion of the state without a fight, Nancy's father still worried about invasion by Confederate raiders.

"It's hard to believe that a year has passed since the war started," she said.

"It seems like more than a year since my life *ended*," Stella commented bitterly. "A year ago we were rich and happy. Today we're poor and miserable. I hate this war and the trouble it's brought us."

Nancy had been through this before with her friend, and she wanted to retort, "The Southerners started it." But she knew that Stella's life was miserable. Although she was tired of hearing her friend's complaints, Nancy wouldn't add to Stella's misery.

Mr. Danford had eventually reclaimed their home, but most of their furniture was gone, and they were living in dangerous and impoverished conditions. Mr. Danford was operating his factory on a small scale, using the hoard of raw cotton he had stored before the war. But lacking a steady supply of cotton, the output wasn't half what it had been prior to their disastrous flight from Wheeling. Because cotton goods were scarce in Wheeling, residents didn't let their dislike of Mr. Danford's Confederate sympathies keep them from buying his products. They needed to replenish their sheets, towels, and clothing.

Even so, the Danfords' lifestyle had changed completely. They couldn't afford any household servants, and new clothes were a thing of the past. Stella and her mother wore the clothing they had taken with them on their aborted flight at the beginning of the war.

"Although it's against his conviction,"

Stella continued morosely, "and he feels like a traitor, Papa got a Union flag and put it on the front porch. He did it for Mama and me. But the local residents know what we believe, and rowdies file past our home about every night shouting and calling us bad names. They're still throwing rotten eggs and vegetables at the house, too."

"The Fosters are having similar problems. Heath is happy to fly the flag because he's a loyal Union man, but he's still harassed because he doctors secessionists. Since that new doctor moved into town from the eastern panhandle, Heath has lost a lot of patients. Even Papa sympathizes with him, so that may be why he insisted that I go back to work for the Fosters."

Stella slanted a sly glance toward Nancy. "And you've been a lot happier since then, too. I wish I had a beau as handsome as Dr. Foster."

Nancy felt her face growing warm, and she didn't answer. Her feelings for Heath were too precious to share with anyone, even her best friend. Stella had assumed the reason she had stopped working for the Fosters was because Pa feared that the Fosters' secessionist sympathies might cause him to lose his hauling contracts with the Union Army. Nancy hadn't corrected her assumptions.

"Dr. Foster is a fine man," Stella continued. "He comes to see Mama every week, and he knows that Papa doesn't have much money to pay him. I'm glad your pa came to his senses about the Fosters."

"So am I. Pa would never admit it, but I think he realizes now what Heath and his mother are going through. Pa is as loyal to the Union as Abe Lincoln himself, but just because my brother is in the Confederate Army, a lot of people shun us. And the army has stopped giving him any shipping business, so we don't have much money, either."

The two girls walked in silence, and Nancy recalled how miserable she'd been during the two months and eleven days she hadn't gone to the Foster home. Being unable to see Heath was about the worst thing that had happened to her, and she moped around the house day after day. Her pa must have thought the same thing, for one morning in February, out of the blue, he said, "If you want to go back to the Fosters, it's all right with me. I'll go with you to see Mrs. Foster tomorrow morning."

Without questions or reservations, Mrs. Foster had welcomed Nancy back. They didn't ask why she had stopped working for them, but she figured Heath suspected the reason. Nancy missed their rides and talks together, but Heath didn't touch her or seek her company unless his mother was present.

Interrupting Nancy's musings, Stella said, "Papa has heard that there's going to be an attack on the Clark home tonight. Now that Mrs. Clark's two brothers have sneaked out of town and joined the Confederate Army, she's suspected of being a spy. People are saying that when she left Tommy with the housekeeper and was gone three days last week, she took information about what's going on in Wheeling to her brothers. There's a rumor flying around that they will guide an army in here to take over the town."

"That's probably a bunch of nonsense. I don't believe Mrs. Clark is brave enough to do that. But because the Union seems to be losing the war, even Pa is fretting what will happen to us if the Confederacy wins. Virginia troops will take over our town if they possibly can and treat us like traitors."

"I hope not," Stella said. "I don't wish that on anyone — not even the people who've been mean to us."

Nancy had long ago forgiven Tabitha Clark for the way she'd treated her, and on her way home, she wondered if she should go and warn Mrs. Clark about the planned attack. Still, the woman had ordered Nancy and Pa to get out of her house and warned them to stay away. Nancy wasn't quite brave enough to risk her anger alone, but she was determined to tell Pa about it. He would know the right thing to do.

Nancy placed a dish of white beans, a platter of corn bread, and a bowl of chopped onions on the table. She took a chair beside her father and waited until he said the blessing.

Her father didn't like to talk as he ate, so Nancy fidgeted until he ate two bowls of beans and onions with several chunks of corn bread. When he pushed back from the table and held up his cup for a coffee refill, she said, "Stella has heard that a mob is going after Mrs. Clark tonight."

As was his way, Pa looked at Nancy to see if she had finished. When she didn't speak, he threaded his graying hair with his fingers, none too clean after a day's work in the shop.

"Don't surprise me. She's too uppity and makes enemies of the wrong people."

"I reckon she's got a right to her own beliefs same as anybody else."

Pa nodded agreement. He never mentioned Clay's name unless Nancy brought up the subject, but when he sat on the steps for several hours in the evening, looking eastward as if he was trying to see what was going on beyond the mountains, Nancy was convinced he was thinking of his son. She figured that was one reason he had mellowed toward the secessionists.

"I thought about warning her, but I didn't want to cause you any trouble."

Knowing that her father would give serious consideration to such a touchy situation before he made a decision, Nancy started clearing the table. She stored the leftovers and then washed and dried the dishes and placed them in the cupboard before she sat at the table again.

"It's a problem, all right, and I don't rightly know what to do about it," her father said. "I don't like the woman because she's too highfalutin, and I fault her for the way she treated you. But I don't like hoodlums, either — 'specially when they prey on a woman and a boy. Wonder if she's the kind to defend herself."

"There's a rack of guns in the hallway. I suppose they belonged to her husband, but I don't know if she can use them."

Pa took his hat from the coatrack beside the door and jammed it on his head. "The Good Book says we're supposed to do good

to them that despitefully use us, so I'm goin'
to help the woman."

"I want to go, too."

"You might as well," Pa said. "I don't
know when I'll be back, and you ain't got
no business bein' alone." He took a shotgun
off the wall, stuck a handful of shells in his
pocket, and reached in a cabinet drawer for
a pistol.

"You'd better take the handgun," he said.
"Your brother taught you how to shoot it,
didn't he?"

"Yes."

"It's just for your protection, mind you. I
don't want you shootin' at nobody unless
you're forced into it. We'll wait till dusk to
go. I don't want to be seen totin' all of this
hardware along the streets."

Frogs croaked along the riverbank, and a
slight breeze wafted the scent of wild plum
blossoms from the island. The sound of a
bugle carried on the night air brought
memories of her brother. As they started
out on their warlike mission, Nancy wondered if her father was thinking of Clay, too.

"It's hard to believe that evil is afoot on
such a nice night," Nancy murmured, and
her father nodded.

"Step lively," he said.

Pa stopped when they were a block from the Clark home. "We'd better go to the back door. I'd like to talk to someone other than the widow first. Does she have any live-in help?"

"I've heard that Nora Lively, one of her poor relations, came to live with her after I left."

"It's worth checkin' out," he said, circling the house to the backyard.

A light still burned in the kitchen, and the curtains were drawn, but they detected movement as if someone moved back and forth in the room. Motioning for Nancy to stay in the background, Pa strode up on the porch and tapped softly on the door.

The door opened slightly, and a quavering voice asked, "Who is it?"

"Wendell Logan," he said quietly. "I want to talk to Mrs. Clark right away. I've come peacefully."

She quickly closed the door and locked it.

"You think she'll talk to you?" Nancy asked.

"I don't know." Pa stared into the darkness that had settled over the city.

"It's too quiet to suit me. If she don't show up soon, we're gettin' out of here."

The door opened a few inches. "You're not welcome here, Mr. Logan," Mrs. Clark said in her haughtiest voice.

"That may be, but Nancy heard today that your house is gonna be attacked tonight. We came to help."

Tabitha peered into the darkness. Nancy moved so she could be seen in the dim light from the kitchen.

"A likely story! Do you think I'd trust you after the way you talked to me?"

Pa stepped forward, shoved on the door, pushed Mrs. Clark aside, and walked into the kitchen. He motioned for Nancy to follow him.

"Leave my house at once."

Pa ignored her and strode toward the front of the house. "It may be a false alarm, but a lot of secessionists are being attacked now, and you being without menfolk, I ain't gonna stand by and see a bunch of riffraff burn your house. Men that attack and pillage in the night are usually cowards, and if they see you're not alone, that might scare them off."

"Take charge, then," Mrs. Clark said meekly.

"Where's your boy?" Pa asked as he walked through the hallway.

"Upstairs in his room."

"Good. That's the safest place for him."

In the dim candlelight, Nancy saw a

woman huddled on the stairway, wringing her hands and moaning. Her father must have sensed that she wouldn't be any help, for he said to Mrs. Clark, "Send her to stay with the boy."

"Nora, please go upstairs and look after Tommy. Don't let him out of his room."

The distraught woman jumped to her feet and scurried up the steps.

To Pa, Mrs. Clark said, "He likes to think he's the man of the house, but he's only eight and a sickly child at that."

"You're right to protect your own," Pa said. With Tommy's safety taken care of, Pa laid out his plans.

"Nancy, be sure the back door is locked, then open the window and watch for anybody who comes up the alley." To Mrs. Clark, he said, "I'm not aimin' to shoot nobody, but it won't hurt to be prepared. Do you know how to shoot any of them guns hanging on the wall?"

"One of them."

"Then load up and be ready. Keep a candle burning so we can see to move around inside, but blow out the other lights. Set by an open window. I'll be out on the front porch, and if I open fire, shoot up in the air. You, too, Nancy," he called quietly. "Be sure you don't hit nobody unless they rush the house."

"Shouldn't the police know about this?" Mrs. Clark asked.

"They're all pro-Union and would likely refuse to help."

"Rather than fighting for a lost cause, I can't understand why my brothers didn't realize that they were needed here," she said in a harsh, raw voice. "We're going to lose everything — our business, our wealth, our homes."

"So you don't think the Confederates will win the war?" Pa asked, and he sounded surprised.

"How can they? The North has railroads, factories, money. Southerners have slaves, cotton, and bravado, none of which is worth much in fighting a war. I sympathize with the secessionists, but old Abe Lincoln has the determination of a bulldog, and he won't give up. Unfortunately, I couldn't make my brothers realize that. Our boats are sitting idle while they're off fighting."

In a tone Nancy had never heard from Mrs. Clark, she added, "Mr. Logan, in light of our past differences, much of which was my fault, I truly appreciate your help tonight. Most of my neighbors don't feel kindly toward me because of my secessionist views. I don't know what I would have done without you and Nancy tonight. I'm thankful you came." She extended her hand, and Pa grasped it without hesitation.

"You've got a right to your political beliefs same as anyone else. Just because I don't believe the same as you do won't keep me from doing what I can to protect you and your boy."

In a trembling voice, Mrs. Clark said, "Whatever happens tonight, I won't forget your kindness."

Pa stepped out on the porch, and quietness settled over the house. Nancy scurried to her post in the kitchen and monitored the passage of time by the clock on the wall. When it struck midnight, as if that was a signal for action, she saw two men sneaking up the alley.

Nancy stepped into the hallway. "Mrs. Clark, tell Pa they're coming the back way," she said. Her heart was hammering, but it was gratifying to know that her voice sounded normal.

Mrs. Clark turned from her post at one of the windows. "And I see a small group of men coming up the street, too. Some of them are carrying torches. Be careful."

At that moment, Nancy saw Tabitha Clark in a new light. If she had thought about it, she would have guessed that Mrs. Clark would be cringing in a corner with her head covered. But there was a steel edge to her voice, and Nancy was convinced that the woman wouldn't hesitate to fire the gun she held if anyone tried to enter the house. Despite her other faults, the woman loved her son devotedly, and she would fight for him like a lioness defending her cub.

The two men moved from the alley, and Nancy heard their steps on the back porch. They pushed on the door, and Nancy turned in that direction, her back against the kitchen wall. If there was any shooting, she figured Pa should start it, but she pushed the pistol in front of her and held it with a steady hand. If the men tried to break in, she would fire.

She moved closer to the door and heard a man's voice mumble, "Pry it open with the crowbar, and don't make no noise."

God, what should I do? I don't want to kill anyone, Nancy thought.

Suddenly she remembered when Heath had told his neighbor that if someone tried to break into the house and harm his mother and Nancy, he wouldn't hesitate to defend them.

Recalling that was enough for Nancy. She tilted the pistol and without warning pulled the trigger. The wood at the top of the door splintered, and one of the men yelled. She was sure she hadn't hit him, so the surprise must have caused him to shout. Nancy stood to one side of the door in case they returned her fire. But no shot sounded, and the men must have thrown the crowbar away, for it hit the side of the house. She heard the rapid beat of footsteps leaving the porch.

As if her shot was a signal, a barrage of gunfire sounded from the street.

"Are you all right, Nancy?" Mrs. Clark called.

"Yes. I shot through the door and scared the attackers away."

For the time being, Nancy decided the back door was safe. She scurried into the front hall and peered out a small window near the place Mrs. Clark knelt.

"So far, they've been shooting in the air," she said quietly.

"I haven't heard Pa's gun. I figure he's mad because I fired, but a couple of men were trying to break in through the kitchen door."

"Hey, secesh," a voice taunted. "You want a quick trip to the Confederacy? We'll ride you out of town on a rail."

Coarse laughter greeted his remark. No doubt this attack was fueled by liquor, for in spite of the town's efforts to control the sale and use of alcohol, it was still available. A man separated from the crowd milling in the street and started toward the house.

When he put his foot on the bottom step, Pa shouted, "That's far enough," and unloaded a volley of shotgun pellets to the right of where the man stood. "The next load of grapeshot will be for real. Get out of here."

"There's only one man — we can take care of him," the man on the step shouted.

Mrs. Clark fired. Pa's gun sounded again, and the advance halted as the attackers huddled together, talking angrily in the middle of the street. Nancy opened a window, knelt beside it, and braced herself for another attack.

Heath yawned, tempted to stop the horse and take a nap in his buggy. He had been at a farmhouse ten miles out in the country for several hours, his patient in labor. Now the baby was delivered, the mother was resting, and he was finally on his way home. He shook his head, slapped his cheeks lightly, relaxed his shoulders, and kept going.

When he arrived in town and drove down Twelfth Street, he noticed a glow a few blocks away. He halted the horse and heard the sound of gunfire. Heath had a sense of uneasiness about what was going on. The Clark home was down that street, and pressure was being put on all secessionists right now. Heath pumped the reins, and the horse picked up speed.

As he drew closer, Heath saw the men milling in front of Tabitha's home. He knew that she and Tommy were alone, with only a weakling cousin for company. A shotgun blast echoed over the street, but he couldn't tell if it came from the house or from the attackers.

He lifted the reins, and with a silent apology to the horse, which had also had a long day and night, he touched its flanks with the whip.

"Giddyup," he yelled, flicking the reins and heading straight toward the rabble. Unaccustomed to the sting of the whip, the horse lunged into action and plowed through the middle of the mob. A few men were knocked down by the wheels, but most of them dove to safety when they saw the buggy bearing down on them. By the time Heath slowed the animal and turned around, the street was empty.

Nancy hurried out on the porch just as Pa stood up, took off his hat, and tossed it into the air. He burst into laughter. "I don't believe I've ever seen a funnier sight. They scattered like a covey of quail."

"Who ran them down, Pa?"

"I don't know. Everything happened so fast, I couldn't take it all in. Whoever it is has turned the vehicle and is coming our way."

Cradling the gun under his arm, Pa walked off the porch.

"Why, it's Doc Foster!" he said.

Heath halted his horse and jumped out of the buggy. "What's going on here?"

"Not much. But there might have been a lot of action if you hadn't arrived when you did." Pa grabbed Heath's hand and pumped it up and down. "You're all right, Doc. You're all right."

As soon as the ruffians had scattered and Heath had come to help, Nancy hurried to the kitchen to light the oil lamp. Now that Pa knew Heath wasn't a coward and would fight when forced into it, a glad song sang in her heart. Would Pa be less concerned about her relationship with Heath?

Surprised not only by his own action but to find Wendell Logan defending the Clark home, Heath stepped inside the hallway. Mrs. Clark hurried out of the parlor and, with a glad cry, ran to Heath, threw her arms around him, and laid her head on his shoulder.

"Oh, I might have known you would come to help me," she cried.

Before Heath could extricate himself from her embrace, he heard footsteps approaching. He looked to the rear of the hallway just as Nancy entered, carrying a lighted lamp. She stopped abruptly and stared. Her features contorted with shock and anger, soon replaced by a look of disappointment and sadness. She set the lamp on a long table and brushed by Heath and Mrs. Clark.

"Let's go home, Pa," she said in a resigned voice. "We aren't needed here any longer."

With Mrs. Clark still holding him tightly, Heath watched the Logans walk away from the house. He removed himself from her arms and turned to follow Nancy.

"Mama, are you all right?" Tommy called from the top of the stairs in a tearful voice.

Mrs. Clark went to the stairway and motioned for Tommy. He ran to her, and she hugged him.

"Everything is all right now. Thanks to the Logans and Dr. Foster."

"I wanted to help, but I don't feel good."

Knowing that Tommy was a fragile child, Heath decided he had better check the boy's heart before he left. Innately, he realized that this wasn't the time to talk to Nancy. In that brief moment when Nancy had found him in Mrs. Clark's embrace, a range of emotions that he hadn't seen there before had flitted across her face. Was it possible that Nancy loved him? With a sigh of resignation, he walked out to his buggy and picked up his medical bag. He would have to mend his fences with Nancy at a later time.

Twelve

Between the late hour when she went to bed and the sleeplessness that plagued her when she thought of Mrs. Clark in Heath's arms, Nancy overslept the next morning. The scent of coffee awakened her. She jumped out of bed, washed hurriedly, struggled into her clothes, and went to the kitchen. Her father was at the table, eating a bowl of oatmeal.

"Sorry, Pa."

"I wanted you to sleep as long as you could. I ain't gonna do much today. I was proud of you last night. If you hadn't guarded the back door, the outcome might have been a lot different."

Flustered over this unexpected praise, Nancy stammered, "I expect Mrs. Clark won't be too happy with me for splintering the door."

"I ain't so sure. She struck me as bein' a lot more sensible than I credited her with. I would have expected her to throw a fit and crawl under a bed when the mob attacked. Instead, she shot into the street. She didn't touch a man, but her shot scattered them. Then the doc added the final touch."

"Is it likely that the mob knows that you and I were there? Will this cause us trouble?" Nancy asked, thinking how ironic it would be for the Logans to be further harassed because they'd helped, of all people, Tabitha Clark.

"I don't know, and I don't care. It's time the citizens of this town remembered that we're all Americans and stops labeling people as traitors because they have family members fightin' on the other side."

"You'd better be careful saying things like that. Now that the army has taken over the Athenaeum Building for a military prison, people considered disloyal to the Union are being put away. I don't want you to end up in prison. Heath goes there to see patients, and he says that the conditions are terrible."

"And he's gonna end up in jail, too, if he don't stop doctorin' the enemy. I've heard threats agin' him," Pa said. "I remember you saying that the Widow Clark was makin' up to Doc Foster. I figure that's all on her side. I notice he didn't take kindly to her throwin' her arms around him last night.

He looked kinda taken aback — she probably hadn't done that before. The woman's barkin' up the wrong tree. She needs a forceful man to curb her spirit — not a meek man like the doc."

Her father's words encouraged Nancy, who had dreaded encountering Heath. But after her father's assessment of the situation, she forced herself to meet Heath as usual, and the incident faded into the background during the increasing lawlessness and unrest that continued to plague the city.

Feeling guilty, although he hadn't done anything to encourage Tabitha Clark, Heath delayed approaching Nancy for a few days, but he could sense her displeasure with him. Finally, he decided he couldn't let the incident pass without comment. But how could he indicate to Nancy that the infatuation was wholly on Mrs. Clark's side and not appear egotistic? Glancing out his office window, Heath saw his mother disappearing down the street, carrying a meal to a soldier's impoverished family. Deciding to face the issue, he hurried across the small section of lawn that separated his office and the house. Nancy was in the kitchen, washing dishes.

Needing to keep his hands busy while he explained, he lifted a dish towel and picked up a plate to dry. Over and over, Heath had debated the best way to broach the subject with Nancy, and he wasn't particularly comfortable with his decision when he said, "I expect you to keep this information in confidence, but Tommy Clark's health isn't good. He has a weak heart, and his mother sends for me many times when the boy isn't really sick. Because of his condition, I can't refuse to go there. I never know when he might have an attack, and it's only for Tommy's sake that I go to her house."

He put the plate he had dried in the cupboard and looked directly at her. "Do you understand?"

"Yes," she murmured, and her lids lowered until he couldn't read the expression in her eyes, but a tender bond of affection escalated between them. He stepped behind her and placed his hands lightly on her shoulders.

"I did nothing to invite Tabitha's embrace that night. I've been attentive to the woman out of pity because I know she may lose her son, but there is nothing more between us — at least on my part. Do you believe me?"

Nancy's heart was singing, and she knew how easy it would be to make a slight turn and be in his arms. She had a feeling he wouldn't reject her if she did, but she wouldn't stoop to Mrs. Clark's tricks.

She nodded her understanding. He squeezed her shoulders and stepped away.

"It's starting to rain again," Nancy complained as she set food on the table for their evening meal. She jumped as a blast of thunder sounded nearby and a streak of lightning illuminated the kitchen.

Her father didn't answer as he filled his plate. No answer was needed. And it wasn't even news, for it had been raining for weeks. They had watched the river for several days as muddy water overflowed its banks and inched closer to their home. They'd lived in this house fifteen years, and the water had never reached the second floor, but no one could tell what the Ohio River might do.

While they ate, the rain increased steadily until it sounded as if buckets of water were being dumped on the house. The wind whistled around the eaves. When Nancy peered out the front window through the haze of rain streaming over it, she saw whitecaps on the river that looked like the waves of the Atlantic Ocean she had seen pictured in one of Heath's books. Willow trees along the riverbank bent double from the force of the wind and dipped their branches into the muddy Ohio.

Her father finished his meal and came to stand by her side. After one look, he galvanized into action. He pulled on a pair of gum boots and took a raincoat from a rack by the door.

"I'm gonna check on the *Wetzel*. The way that water is churnin', the boat might be set adrift. And if it breaks loose, I want to be on it."

"Oh, Pa, be careful!"

He nodded, pulled a hat firmly on his head, and hurried out the door.

Feeling the need to keep busy, Nancy cleared the dishes from the table and washed them. She had just finished and was hanging the dishcloth and towel behind the stove to dry when the persistent ringing of the bell on the top deck of the *Wetzel* caused her heart to skip a beat.

Pa was in trouble, or he wouldn't be ringing the bell like that. Pausing only long enough to put on a coat and hat, Nancy ran through the rain, sloshing through water puddles that soaked her shoes and stockings before she got to the river.

She raced up the gangplank of the *Wetzel*.

"Pa! What is it? Where are you?"

He shouted from the pilothouse, but she

couldn't hear what he said. She took the steps to the hurricane deck two at a time.

"What's wrong? I thought the *Wetzel* was adrift," she shouted. When she reached her father, he was leaning against the railing, peering through the mist and rain.

Her eyes followed his pointing hand. "See that boat? It has run aground, and there's a heap of men on it. It's probably the one from Pittsburgh bringing soldiers to join the army in Parkersburg. The pilot must be a stranger to this part of the river and didn't know about the sandbar that makes the eastern channel too shallow for navigation. Or maybe the buoy washed away in the storm. You keep ringin' the bell while I run uptown to get help."

Nancy's arm was tired of ringing the bell by the time several wagonloads of men arrived on the riverbank. Gradually, the strength of the storm lessened as it moved eastward. The steamboat was floundering in the waves generated by the aftermath of the storm. Men were diving from the sinking boat and swimming toward the bank. Those on shore helped them up the slippery bank. Nancy saw her father approaching the *Wetzel,* and she hurried to meet him at the gangplank.

"Was anybody drowned?"

"The boat's captain says they're all safe. Since they landed on that sandbar, the water was shallow, and most of them waded ashore. But a few are wounded, so I sent a man after Doc Foster."

"Thank God they weren't all killed."

Shouting from the doomed boat intensified. Nancy looked toward the accident scene just as the boat toppled into the deepest channel of the river.

Pa shook his head. "Poor fellers! They lost all of their gear and their supplies. I suppose they'll have to stay here until they get some equipment."

"And the camp already has more soldiers than they can handle."

"Could you rustle up something for them to eat and drink?"

Aghast, Nancy turned to him. "How many are there?"

"I counted about forty."

"Forty!"

Nancy stared at her pa, but when he didn't act as if he'd made an unreasonable request, she said, "I'll see what I can find," and hurried off the steamboat.

"What can I fix in a hurry?" Nancy mumbled as she rushed toward the house, bending her head against the wind that still held some rain. "I'd better get hot water to boiling first so I can make coffee."

After she filled a teakettle and a big pot with water and set them on the stove, she hurried down to the cellar. She always laid by enough goods in stone jars to last for a year, so she put two jars of pickled peaches and a chunk of smoked ham in a basket. When she came out of the cellar, Mrs. Foster was walking toward the house. Nancy hurried toward her.

"I've never been so glad to see anyone in my life. Pa asked me to fix something for the shipwrecked soldiers to eat. We don't have enough food in the house to feed that many men."

Mrs. Foster squeezed Nancy's shoulders. "When I heard what had happened, I came with Heath to see if anyone needed nursing. He says that none of the men have severe injuries. I wasn't needed there, and your father asked me to come give you a hand."

"I made two loaves of bread yesterday, and we can make sandwiches with this ham, but that won't be a drop in the bucket to feed so many."

"We won't have to do it all by ourselves. Soldiers have arrived from the island. The army cook has started a fire, and he's making coffee. Two island women rowed across with their men, and they went home to

173

prepare some food, too. Just like when Jesus fed the five thousand — we'll have food left over when they're all fed."

Mrs. Foster and Nancy were used to working together, and Mrs. Foster soon adjusted to the more primitive conditions in the Logan kitchen. In a short time, they filled two large baskets with sandwiches and slices of cake that Nancy had made the day before. They covered the baskets with pieces of oilcloth to keep the intermittent rain from spoiling the food. After they prepared a large peach cobbler and put it in the oven to bake, they carried the baskets to the riverbank.

Pa saw them coming and hurried to take the basket from Mrs. Foster's hands. "That was quick," he said approvingly.

"I see they already have tents set up," Mrs. Foster said.

"Yes, ma'am. One is for the cook, and one for the doc to check out the wounded. The officer in charge at the army camp has already sent a detachment to find six or seven tents. They ought to have them in the clothing factory that's makin' uniforms and other army supplies. They're goin' to be here a spell, for they lost everything."

Nancy handed her basket to a young soldier dressed in homespun garments, whose only sign that he was a soldier was the short-billed, blue Union cap he wore. His wet clothes clung to his slender body, and he shivered in spite of the humid air. His face was a mask of fear and pain. He didn't appear to be more than twelve or thirteen years old, and Nancy wondered why he had ever enlisted in the army.

Mrs. Foster's eyes, too, were full of pity as she surveyed the discouraged men. She motioned to the two island women who had arrived with baskets of food. When they joined Nancy and her, Mrs. Foster said, "We need to do something for these soldiers. If you can organize the women on the island to gather up items for them, I'll get my friends and neighbors to do the same."

"What'd you have in mind?" Nancy asked.

"The army will provide clothes and blankets for them. We can gather soap, towels, needles and thread, and medication and put them in cloth sacks that they could carry along when they leave. We could make cookies, too."

"Maybe we can find a few Bibles," Nancy said. "I know we won't be able to get a Bible for everyone, but they can share."

"This ain't gonna be a short war, to my thinking," one of the women said. "Let's keep up this good work even after we send these men on their way."

"That's an excellent plan," Mrs. Foster said and shook hands with the two women. "God will reward you for your goodness. Nancy, why don't you come home with me, and we'll organize my neighbors to help."

"I'll ask Pa."

Within a week, the soldiers were on their way eastward to an uncertain destiny, but Nancy believed they were encouraged by the attention they'd received from the women of Wheeling. She joined a large crowd at the depot to cheer them on the way, pleased that the misfortune of those soldiers had encouraged her and other local women to help needy servicemen and their families.

THIRTEEN

Throughout the summer, drunkenness in the city of Wheeling increased lawlessness to the point where her father wouldn't let Nancy go anywhere, day or night, unescorted. The city council passed an ordinance prohibiting the sale of liquor to soldiers, who devised all sort of plans to smuggle booze into the camp on the island. Pa didn't mention it to her, but Nancy learned from her friends that after the city passed an ordinance suppressing houses of prostitution, many of the women had taken refuge at the army camp. Pa relied increasingly on Mrs. Foster to provide a safe environment for her.

Nancy often wondered if either of their parents was aware of the emotional bond that was growing steadily between Heath and her. Or did they approve of a closer relationship? After that night on the *Wetzel,* Pa hadn't mentioned again that Heath was an unfit suitor for her, and she welcomed every moment she spent with Heath and his mother.

"Mother," Heath said one evening when the Fosters and Nancy were enjoying a quiet time together after their evening meal. "The city authorities are cracking down on a lot of lawlessness among the soldiers, but I wonder if they aren't going about it the wrong way."

Mrs. Foster removed her glasses and looked up from the socks she was knitting.

"What does thee have in mind?"

"Is it ever satisfactory to meet force with force? Jesus taught that we're to do good to all men. Every week, trains come into Wheeling from Illinois and Ohio, transporting soldiers to the battlefields. Many of them are hardly more than boys. I'm sure they're scared and homesick, and that may be the reason they get drunk and disorderly."

"It is quite a problem, though, for liquor is easy to get," Nancy said. "Pa has heard that farmers hide spirits in the hay or straw carried on the wagons they take to the army camp, and grocers sneak in liquor when they're taking supplies. Besides, people back in the hills make moonshine and sell it to the soldiers. When Pa is home, he hardly ever sleeps at night but keeps going back and forth between the house and the *Wetzel.* That's the reason I stay over here so much. He says he can't protect me and our property, too."

Mrs. Foster smiled fondly at Nancy. "You've become an important part of our household. I don't know what we'd do without you." She turned to Heath. "If these young men don't have something positive to do, they are bound to get into trouble. And several families in this town are in need, too. Husbands and fathers have gone off to war, leaving their families destitute. The soldiers send money home when they can, but they don't get paid regularly, and that leads to stealing. Our sewing circles are busy making clothes. But what else can we do?"

While Heath deliberated, Nancy said, "I don't know what we can do for the ones in the army camp, but a lot of the soldiers from the West just stop over in Wheeling for a few hours. Why couldn't we set up a welcome center down at the station and give them coffee and cake?"

"That would be a good start," Heath approved. "With our industry disrupted like it is, I'm sure there are some empty warehouses you could use."

The next day, Nancy and Mrs. Foster formulated plans to add entertaining these soldiers to their activities. They also enlisted the help of Tabitha Clark, who, since the time Nancy and her father had come to her rescue, had joined the women's sewing circles. Pa had commented, "That doesn't surprise me. Widow Clark has lots of possibilities — she just needed to wake up."

Nancy was happy to be helping the Union soldiers, but she often remembered Clay, wondering if Confederate women were providing his needs.

Heath entered the portals of the Federal Court Building and joined a line of other citizens who had been summoned to appear before the judge to answer to charges of disloyalty.

Lord, he prayed silently, *my attitude is wrong. Give me the grace to speak as Thou would have me speak — that I might not answer hostility with hostility. Help me to be gracious even as Thou wast in the midst of persecution.*

He had been astounded two days ago when he had received the summons to appear in court. He supposed he shouldn't have been surprised, because he had been aware that citizens were no longer judged on their past contributions. There was no middle ground — either you took an oath of allegiance, or you were a traitor.

He had taken the oath of allegiance months earlier, and the Union flag was displayed on a staff on his front porch. But in the patriotic fervor of the moment and with the fear of Confederate invasion, past performances counted for little. Other pacifists had been harassed, so now it was his time.

The men in line didn't exchange glances with anyone else, and talking was subdued and at a minimum. No one wanted to be here, nor did they want to be seen in this company. Heath's turn came at last. He stood before the judge, who riffled some papers on his desk and looked up.

"Dr. Foster, my apologies for calling you away from your humanitarian work, which is well-known in the area. However, charges of disloyalty have been brought against you. I'm sure you will agree that in these troubled times, it is imperative for this court to examine all accusations."

"Even when the charges are unfounded?"

The judge turned steely eyes upon Heath. "That is for the court to decide." He looked again at his papers and handed a sheet to

Heath. "This is an oath of allegiance that all male citizens are required to sign."

"Which I signed several months ago."

"Some revisions have been made in the oath."

Heath was aware of the changes, and he had no intention of signing the paper, but he scanned it quickly. The only change from the previous oath was the addition of the words, "and will neither directly nor indirectly give aid or information to the enemies of the United States, and will not advocate or sustain, either in public or private, the cause of the so-called Confederate states."

Heath handed the paper back to the judge, who refused to take it.

"I won't sign this paper. If I did, it would supersede the Hippocratic oath I signed when I became a physician. I refer to the words, 'I will apply dietetic measures for the benefit of the sick according to my ability and judgment; I will keep them from harm and injustice. . . . Whatever houses I may visit, I will come for the benefit of the sick.' "

The judge's expression was stern, his voice sarcastic. "I'm sure the famed Hippocrates would have held the defense of his beloved Greece higher than his devotion to the sick."

In Heath's opinion, this comment didn't

deserve an answer. Instead he said, "But from the Holy Bible, I have a mandate that supersedes my medical oath. Jesus indicated that His people would be those who fed the hungry and helped the stranger. I have particularly heeded His words, 'I was sick and ye visited me: I was in prison and ye came unto me.' He ministered to Samaritans and Romans, as well as Jews, and if confronted with our present crisis, I'm sure our Lord wouldn't have made a difference between Union and secessionists in His healing ministry."

The judge's eyes were cold and proud, and he continued as if he hadn't heard Heath. "I understand that you have visited the homes of many secessionists, which has caused suspicion, and that you go to the prison to treat Confederate soldiers. How does anyone know whether you went to treat the sick or to discuss treasonous measures toward our nation?"

"When they need medical attention, a Confederate sympathizer or a Unionist looks alike to me."

"You still refuse to sign?"

Heath dipped a pen in the inkwell the judge pushed toward him, scratched out the words that offended him, signed the paper, and gave it back to him. The judge scrutinized the form.

"You may go now, Doctor, but your activities will be watched."

Heath expected to be arrested every time he attended a person who was known to favor the Southern cause, but the months passed and no one challenged his activities. He wondered if he was spared because of his mother's humanitarian help to soldiers and their families. If his mother helped Confederate sympathizers, he didn't want to know.

FOURTEEN

Nancy slipped her hand in her pocket as she and her father walked home from worship Sunday morning. Looking for a handkerchief, she was surprised to feel a piece of paper instead. Intuition told her it was a note, for she knew the paper hadn't been there earlier. She had no idea when or by whom it had been placed in her pocket. Heart pounding, Nancy hurried up the stairs and into her room, closing the door behind her. She pulled the paper from her pocket and unfolded it.

I'm hurt bad and don't know if I'm gonna make it. I've been travelin' for weeks, wantin' to get home before I died. I know Pa wouldn't want me to come home, so I'm hidin' in Wetzel's Cave. You know where it is. I'd like to see you.

The message wasn't signed, and although

the writing was hard to decipher, she was sure it was from Clay. It had been thirteen months since he had left home, and this was the first message they'd had from him for almost three months.

She hadn't been there for several years, but Nancy was well aware of the location of Wetzel's Cave. On a hill overlooking Wheeling Creek, the cave was the legendary home of Lewis Wetzel, a backwoodsman who had roamed the countryside during the latter part of the eighteenth century when settlers first came into the upper Ohio River valley. During her childhood, Nancy had gone to the cave several times with her friends until her father found out about it and abruptly stopped her cave excursions. She wasn't sure she could find the cave now, yet she had to try. But how could she get away without Pa knowing?

That afternoon when her father was contacted by the army to make an unscheduled trip on the *Wetzel,* Nancy thought his departure was divine providence, until he told her to spend the night with Mrs. Foster. But since Mrs. Foster didn't know she was supposed to be there, Nancy could slip away to see Clay without anyone knowing about it. She had to be careful. If the authorities discovered Clay's hiding place, he would be locked up in the military prison, where he would surely die since he was badly wounded. In spite of Heath's efforts to heal the Confederate prisoners, many of them had died.

Nancy packed a basket with food and medicines. She put on heavy shoes and her oldest dress because she would be climbing over rough terrain before she reached the cave. She would stay off the main streets and take alleys until she found the path that she could follow up the hill to the cave. She filled the lantern with oil and settled down to wait for dark, trying to remember the way to the cave.

Loud talking and hilarity across the river told her that someone had smuggled in another batch of liquor. She didn't want to be apprehended by a drunken soldier, so when semidarkness approached, Nancy left home and walked stealthily, all of her senses alert to detect the first sign of danger. She reached the National Road without meeting anyone she knew; she believed her escape was going without a hitch, only to be brought up short when she heard a buggy approaching behind her. She turned quickly. It was Heath, and her shoulders slumped in despair. He halted his horse, looking at her with a probing query in his eyes.

"I noticed that the *Wetzel* was gone and you hadn't come to our home. What are you doing out here?"

After one quick glance at Heath, Nancy looked away, unwilling to meet his eyes. She knew she could trust him, but she didn't want anyone to know where Clay was. Not only would Clay be in danger, but anyone who harbored a Confederate soldier was subject to arrest. Heath was already in enough trouble with the local authorities. Why hadn't she started five minutes earlier and avoided this meeting with him? Tongue-tied, she looked piteously at him.

Gathering the reins in one hand, Heath held out his right hand to her. Torn between uncertainty over what she should do and the relief of confiding in Heath, she took his hand and stepped into the buggy. He gazed curiously at the heavy haversack she dropped at her feet and at the unlighted lantern she carried.

"We'll drive around for a while."

Leaving the thoroughfare, he turned right into the industrial section of Wheeling. He slowed his horse to a slow gait and traveled along a quiet street. When she remained silent for the better part of fifteen minutes, he asked softly, "Is it Clay?"

Nancy nodded, but knowing he probably

couldn't see in the dim streetlights, she said quietly, "Yes." Glad now that she had someone to share her burden, she told him about the note she'd received.

"I didn't know how I could go to Clay without Pa knowing, and I felt like God had arranged for him to leave to give me the opportunity to see my brother." Her lips trembled. "He said he's dying, but I brought some medicines and things to help him if I can."

Heath asked for directions to the cave and turned his horse and buggy. "We'll go home so I can stable the horse, and I'll go with you."

"I don't want you to get into trouble."

"I'm always in trouble. Even if he weren't your brother, I'd try to help him. And if he is dying, you shouldn't have to suffer through it alone."

She knew how dangerous it was for him to come with her; still, his presence would be a comfort. The exigencies of war had made her more self-reliant, but it was heartening to have Heath share her burden. He stabled the horse and asked Nancy to wait in his office. He went into the house and soon returned dressed in a pair of loose trousers and a short wool jacket. He had changed his shoes for a pair of brogans. He carried his medical bag in one hand and balanced the haversack on his shoulder as they set out. Nancy carried the lantern.

"Tell me about this cave."

"There are several caves in the hills around Wheeling, but this particular one was the hideout of Lewis Wetzel, a backwoods scout. Wetzel dedicated his life to protecting the settlers from Indian raids. That's where Pa got the name for his steamboat. When we were children, we played on these hills and in the caves."

"You go first and I'll follow," he said.

"I haven't been to the cave for a long time, but I think I can find it. The path used to be well traveled, but it may be hidden by underbrush now."

Nancy led the way out of town, plunged into the wild plum thicket that concealed the entrance to the path, and headed uphill. Surely God's hand was leading the way, for the path she followed seemed familiar.

Time passed quickly, and when she finally paused for a quick breath, she said, "We're almost there. We go downhill for just a short distance, and we'll find the cave — I'm sure of it."

They approached a large stone slab, and she pointed. "That must be it. This entrance is small, but once we're inside, the cave branches out into several small rooms. We called one of the rooms the hideout. I figure that's where Clay will be."

She crawled through the opening and peered anxiously ahead to where the cave branched into more than one room, but she didn't see anyone. Bending low, Heath entered the cave.

"Wait here," he said. "I'll check everything out first."

Heath gave Nancy a quick embrace as he moved past her and looked into a small room. His head barely cleared the ceiling, but he held the lantern high and glanced around the damp, cool room. The room had a musty smell, but his medical instincts also picked up a fetid stench, the odor of mortifying flesh. Was Nancy too late to see her brother?

"Clay," he called quietly. "Clay Logan, are you here?"

A low, eerie moan was his only answer, but he moved toward the sound. A man lay on his back, covered with a ragged blanket.

"Come on in, Nancy," Heath called.

When she rushed to his side, he said, "There's a man here, and it's probably your brother."

Still hesitant, Nancy moved in the direction Heath indicated and looked down. Heath turned up the wick of the lantern, and she knelt beside the man. Could this emaciated, bearded, dirty man be Clay? But on closer inspection, she looked up, tears glistening in her eyes.

"It's Clay," she said. She touched her brother's arm. "It's Nancy. I've come to help you."

The man tried to sit up but fell back on the dirty pallet. Heath knelt on the other side and found a feeble pulse. He lifted the blanket and replaced it quickly before Nancy saw the blood-soaked garments.

Nancy took a bottle of water from her pack. "If you'll hold him up, I'll give him some water."

Heath carefully lifted Clay into a reclining position and propped him against his knees. Clay groaned and gasped. With a shaking hand, Nancy lifted the bottle to her brother's mouth. She managed to force a few swallows between his parched lips before his head rolled to one side.

Heath lowered him to the ground. "He's passed out. He has a bad wound in his side."

Nancy touched Clay's face. "He's awful hot."

Heath nodded. "His temperature is high. Why don't you wash his face and hands? I'll try to revive him long enough for you to talk to him."

"You think he's going to die?"

Heath looked away so he wouldn't have to see the impact on his beloved when he answered, "Yes."

"I wish Pa was here."

"I'd go after him, but I don't think there's time. The bad odor from his wound indicates that gangrene has set in. If we can rouse him, I'll give him a morphine tablet to dull the pain."

She shook her head. "Pa won't be home until tomorrow morning."

Nancy kept washing her brother's face, and once when he roused, they forced a morphine tablet down his throat. He seemed to sleep after that. Nancy held his hand while Heath sat beside her, his arm around her waist, her head resting on his shoulder.

Once, when the misery in Nancy's heart boiled to the surface and she started crying, Heath wiped away her tears with his handkerchief and kissed her lips softly.

"How I wish I could have spared thee this trouble. Thou art precious to me, and I hate to see thee suffering in this way."

Heath's words gave Nancy the courage to face what problems Clay's return and his death would cause her family. She remembered the time when Mrs. Foster had told her that Quakers used the old form of *you* when they spoke to fellow believers, to close members of the family, or to those they loved. She wasn't a Quaker, and she wasn't a family member, so in this gentle way, when she needed encouragement more than any other time in her life, Nancy knew that Heath loved her.

Clay slept peacefully for an hour, and when he woke up after a bolt of pain seemed to slither through his body, his eyes opened and focused on Nancy and Heath.

"What —," he said. He started to sit up, gasped, and fell back again. Heath put Nancy's knapsack under his head.

"Where am I? What are you doing here, Sis?"

"You're in Wetzel's Cave. I don't know how you got here. I brought Dr. Foster to help you."

Monitoring Clay's pulse, Heath shook his head. Nancy knew that Clay was sinking fast, and if they were to learn what had happened to him, he needed to talk now. "How were you wounded?"

Slowly, with many pauses to catch his breath, Clay gasped out the facts of his injury.

"I've been fighting with one Confederate general after another in northeast Virginia most of the time I've been gone. Mostly, we've been trying to keep control of the B&O Railroad. The Federal troops are better equipped than we are, and it seemed like bad luck plagued us from the first. I was shifted from one unit to another, fighting around Harper's Ferry and other mountain areas. I was hit by sniper fire. The army doctors don't have much to work with, and I didn't get any better. I wanted to come home to die, and another soldier and me headed west. I didn't figure Pa would take me in, so I crawled up here." Turning his attention to Heath, he asked, "How much time do I have, Doc?"

"A few hours."

Clay nodded. "Well, I made my choice. I lived with it, and now I'm a-dyin' with it. I'm not sorry. I could have gotten wounded no matter which army I joined. But the whole war was a big mistake. I see that now. We had a great country. I don't know why we couldn't get along. I did what my commanding officers told me to, but it just didn't seem right to be shooting at other Americans — men who spoke the same language we do, men who worship the same God."

The morphine was having its effect, and he slept again. Heath put his arm around Nancy, and they leaned against the damp walls of the cave. Daylight was seeping into the tunnel when Clay wakened again.

"Nancy," he said, "you know I ain't been too bad. I've always helped out anybody in need. Do you suppose God will have me?"

Knowing she was out of her element when it came to discussing eternal salvation with her brother, Nancy looked helplessly at Heath.

Placing his hand lightly on Clay's forehead, he spoke tenderly, "Spending eternity in heaven with God doesn't depend on the things we have done or haven't done. The way to eternal life was made possible because of what Jesus, God's Son, did when He died on the cross for the sins of all mankind. After we've accepted Jesus as our Savior, then we're expected to live good lives, but there's nothing we can do to save our souls. Jesus took care of that at Calvary."

"Nobody in our company had a whole Bible, but we passed scraps of the New Testament around among us. There was one word I couldn't understand. Somethin' like that Jesus was the propicheation for our sins. Do you know what I'm talkin' about?"

Heath answered softly, "Yes — that's one

of my favorite passages in the book of Romans. 'For all have sinned, and come short of the glory of God; being justified freely by his grace through the redemption that is in Christ Jesus: whom God hath set forth to be a propitiation through faith in his blood, to declare his righteousness for the remission of sins that are past.' *Propitiation* means that through His death, Jesus became the means by which people's sins can be forgiven."

Sweat popped out on Clay's face. Heath felt his pulse and spoke quickly.

"Have you taken that step in your relationship with God? Have you accepted Him as your Savior?"

A beautiful smile momentarily erased the suffering on Clay's face. "I did that a long time ago, Doc."

"Then you need no other assurance that God will indeed have you."

"Tell Pa I'm sorry I disobeyed him and went to fight with the enemy. Do you think he'll forgive me?"

"He already has," Nancy assured her brother. "When you left, he told me never to mention your name to him, but anytime I've had news of you, I've told him, and he was glad to hear."

"I thank God for that." With an effort,

Clay lifted his hand and patted Nancy's cheek. "I've always looked after you, little sister, but now somebody else will have to take care of you." Lowering his hand, he looked significantly at Heath.

Clay lived on until midmorning, but he didn't speak again. Nancy held her brother's left hand; Heath held his right one; and as the minutes passed, they felt life slowly leaving his body. The smile that had spread across Clay's face when he confessed his belief in Jesus as his Savior faded at last.

Nancy lifted her eyes to Heath's. He nodded and drew the blanket over Clay's face. Her brother had moved from this troubled world to a place where he would feel no more pain. After witnessing his hours of suffering, she couldn't be sorry that he had died.

"What do we do now?" she asked quietly.

"I've spent the last hour trying to decide if we should just bury him here in the hills and not tell anyone about his death. If we take his body to be buried in Wheeling, you and your father may be hounded more than you have been."

"I think Pa ought to know — he should make the decision."

"Then one of us will stay with Clay. The

other will go and tell your father."

"I wish you would go and tell him. I don't think I could bear to break the news to him. For all of their differences, Pa and Clay loved each other. He should be home by the time you get there."

"That probably is best, but I don't like to leave you here alone."

"That's the only way."

Heath stood up, saying wearily, "Yes, I suppose it is. I wish I could have spared thee this trouble, my dear."

He came to her and gathered her snugly into his arms. Gently he rocked her back and forth. Softly his breath fanned her face. She pulled back slightly and looked at him. He first kissed her with his eyes, and then she felt his lips on hers as light as a whisper.

"I love thee, Nancy. Dost thou feel the same for me?"

"Forever and ever," she promised softly. He kissed her again and released her.

"I'll be back as soon as I can," he promised and exited the cave.

Nancy felt an immeasurable peace and satisfaction. Perhaps this cave, with her brother lying dead at her feet, was a strange place for Heath and her to declare their love, but she knew Clay wouldn't have minded. She sat down again and removed

the blanket from her brother's face. All
through her life, Clay had been her protec-
tor — now he had given her into Heath's
care.

FIFTEEN

As he hurried away from the cave and made the long walk into town, Heath agonized over what he should do first and how he could approach Wendell about the loss of his son. The *Wetzel* was docked at the foot of the street. As he approached, he saw that the crew was still unloading freight, so they hadn't been in port long.

God, I don't know how to break this news. Give me the wisdom to approach Wendell in the right way about the tragedy that has struck his family.

A deckhand told Heath that Wendell was in his office, and he headed in that direction. Wendell looked up, startled, when Heath tapped on the door. Perhaps Heath's expression warned Wendell that something was wrong, for he clenched the handful of freight bills he held. "Is my girl all right?"

"Oh yes, Nancy is fine," Heath hastily assured him, "but I do have bad news."

He quickly related how Nancy had received the note, how they had gone to the cave, and how Clay had subsequently died.

"Since it's against the law to harbor or give aid to a Confederate soldier or sympathizer, Nancy and I discussed burying Clay in the hills without telling anyone. But she believed that decision should be left up to you."

Wendell dropped the freight bills into a desk drawer, took his hat off the rack, and pulled it low on his forehead. When he started out the door, Heath asked, "What are you going to do?"

"I'm goin' after my boy, that's what! I ain't no Confederate sympathizer, but Clay's my boy. I'm bringin' him home to be buried beside his ma. I'll get my men to build a coffin, and we'll carry him off the hill. If my neighbors don't like it, that's too bad — it won't matter to me." He paused and looked directly at Heath. "I thank you for helpin' Nancy out, but your part don't need to be made public. No need for you to be arrested for aidin' and abettin' the enemy. I'll take it from here."

Heath nodded his thanks. But when Wendell and his deckhands arrived at the cave with the hastily built wooden coffin several hours later, Heath was waiting with Nancy.

And he followed along as the small cortege carried the body of Clay Logan out of the hills and to the cemetery to be buried beside his mother.

The news must have circulated rapidly, for a crowd of more than fifty people had gathered at the cemetery, including Mrs. Foster, Tabitha Clark, and the editor of the *Intelligencer,* Archibald Campbell, to mourn with Nancy and her father. The next day, Heath brought a copy of the newspaper to Nancy.

"I guess Mr. Campbell's editorial has summed up the feelings of most Wheeling residents today," he said as he read the headline: "NATIVE SON DIES FOR HIS COUNTRY."

With tears seeping from her eyes and drizzling over her cheeks, Nancy read,

"Yesterday in Wheeling, a truce was declared. There was no North or South — no Confederates or Yankees. Confederate sympathizers, loyal Union men and women, and grieving neighbors, some with no particular political beliefs, gathered to pay their last respects to Clay Logan, who died for the cause he held dear. All mankind looks the same in God's eyes. The preacher summed up the feeling of Wheeling's citizens yesterday by quoting from the book of Galatians: 'For ye are all the children of God by faith in Christ Jesus. For as many of you as have been baptized into Christ have put on Christ. There is neither Jew nor Greek, there is neither bond nor free, there is neither male nor female; for ye are all one in Christ Jesus.' I applaud those who risked persecution and harassment to honor a fallen soldier."

When Nancy finished reading, Heath pulled her into a close embrace and held her until she stopped crying.

A week after Clay's funeral, Heath brought Nancy home in the buggy, and she asked him to stay for supper. He had a call to make on one of her neighbors, but he promised to return for the evening meal. Nancy was atwitter as she prepared stewed chicken and dumplings, potatoes, and green beans to her satisfaction. The biscuits turned out golden and flaky. She opened a jar of pickled cucumbers. Heath not only complimented her on the meal, but ate as heartily as he did at his own table.

After they finished eating a slice of chocolate cake, Heath pushed back from the table. "Wendell," he said, "I have another call to make soon, but now seems as good a time as any to ask for your permission to court Nancy."

Nancy gasped, and her face flushed. Since the time he had declared his love in the cave where Clay had died, she had felt sure that Heath would approach her father, but she hadn't expected it so soon.

"I realize that Nancy is mourning her brother, so I wouldn't expect to marry right away, but I do love her. I'd like to have your permission to marry her eventually, and to keep company with her until that time."

Wendell took a big swig of coffee and looked from Nancy to Heath.

"And what does Nancy think about that?"

"I didn't want to ask her until I'd discussed it with you, but I'm sure she shares my feelings."

"Nancy?"

She sensed her father's gaze on her, and she knew he would press for an answer. She couldn't lift her head, and she was tongue-tied. The silence grew in the room until she nodded her head and sneaked a quick look at her father. The room seemed deathly still as her father deliberated.

"I know you don't approve of my political beliefs," Heath said, "but I can't understand why that will keep me from being a good husband for Nancy."

"I ain't necessarily agin' this marriage, but there are things to consider. Nancy, look at me. Do you want to marry the doc?"

Nancy lifted her head and unwaveringly met her father's eyes. "Yes."

He nodded and looked at Heath. "I ain't agin' havin' you court, but speakin' as man to man, it might be well for Nancy to get used to the idea gradually."

"I understand what you mean, and as I said, I don't mean to rush into marriage. For one thing, Nancy is sad now about Clay's death, and she should be happy at her wedding."

Nancy flashed a grateful smile in his direction, marveling that he understood her so well.

"Now that I have your permission, I want to build a house. My mother will probably insist that we live with her, but every woman should have her own home. There's an empty lot on the same street where we live, and I've got an option to buy it. Nancy can plan the house the way she wants it, and by the time the house is built, we should be ready to marry."

Her father nodded approvingly and cleared his throat. Nancy noted a mist in his eyes. "You have my blessing."

Nancy walked downstairs with Heath when he rose from the table and shyly received his kiss. As she watched him drive away, Nancy had never been happier. When she returned to the kitchen, her father still sat at the table.

She put her arms around his shoulders. "Thanks, Pa. You've made me very happy."

"He's a good man, and he'll take care of you. I can't ask for more."

Nancy walked slowly along Market Street on her way to the Foster home. The months that had passed since Clay's death had brought death and tragedy to many families in Wheeling, and sadness seemed to hover over the city. The concern about Southern sympathizers in the city had taken second place to the guerilla warfare occurring in the counties west of the Alleghenies. Several raids had been conducted by Virginia raiders determined to block the new state movement and to keep the western counties as part of the Confederacy.

Because Wheeling was the most important city in the west, many of these expeditions attempted to reach their area. Nancy had been worried when the city was placed on alert several times, but so far, none of the guerilla bands had reached Wheeling. The news, however, was disturbing, for while lawmakers continued to make decisions that would eventually change the political map of Virginia, the military outcome seemed to favor the Confederacy.

Sometimes her father worried that the Union might actually lose the war. Once, he'd said to Nancy, "If that happens, we'll have to move into Ohio or farther west. Or maybe Heath will take you back to Philadelphia."

"I don't think so," Nancy said. "He likes it here, and he believes the Union will ultimately win. He takes a lot of magazines and newspapers, and from what he reads, he says that the Union Army is getting stronger — that all they need now is a general who will fight instead of retreating every time they lose a battle."

But in spite of the bad news from the war front and the threat of invasion by Southern troops, Nancy was happy in her love for Heath. Lacking a mother, as soon as Pa gave permission for their eventual marriage, Nancy approached Mrs. Foster for guidance.

"I love Heath very much, but it will take more than that to make me the kind of wife he needs. Working for you has taught me to how to keep house the way he's accustomed to. But I want to improve my mind so I can discuss subjects that interest him. Will you help me?"

"Of course I'll help you. During the winter months, you'll have more time to read. I'll point out his favorite volumes on the bookshelves, and you can read those. By being in our home, you've already learned much about our customs and our ways. I have no doubt that you'll fit graciously into his life. He's made a good choice."

Sixteen

January 1863

Heath let in a cold blast of air when he arrived home from his daily calls. Nancy hurried to help him take off his heavy overcoat, and he bent to kiss her.

"Your face is cold," she protested, but he kissed her anyway, took off his gloves, and placed his cold hands on her face. She shivered.

"It's cold outdoors. All of us can't stay inside where it's warm," he joked.

He waved a copy of the *Intelligencer*. "It's happened at last."

"What has happened?"

He unfolded the paper and read, "In spite of opposition from half of his cabinet, on December 31, President Lincoln signed the bill favoring the admission of West Virginia into the Union."

Entering from the kitchen in time to hear the news, Mrs. Foster said, "It's about time.

It's been months since the statehood bill was introduced by our senators."

"There was a lot of maneuvering back and forth, trying to decide what was legal and what wasn't," Heath agreed. "But after Senator Willey made a proposal last July concerning statehood that was passed by the U.S. Senate, there wasn't much doubt that we would be a separate state. After a lot of deliberation, President Lincoln finally got around to signing the bill."

"Does that mean we're a new state?" Nancy asked.

"Not yet, but we're getting closer. The West Virginia Constitutional Convention will meet to adopt a few changes made to the original proposal; then the voters will have to approve the constitution as amended. It will still be several months."

He put the paper aside. "But enough political discussion," Heath said. "You can read the paper later. It's time to have the plans drawn up for our home, and I want to know what kind of house you want."

"I can't get excited about a new home when the war effort is going against the Union. After the Confederates won the Battle of Fredericksburg in December, everybody expects General Lee to head our way. If the Confederacy wins, the first thing they'll do is retake our counties, and probably those of us who are pro-Union will lose everything we have."

Heath took her hand and led her to a map of the United States on the wall with the state of Virginia highlighted. "You shouldn't fret about that. In the first place, the Confederacy isn't going to win. It's true that they have great generals and valiant soldiers, but the Union does also."

"But the Confederates have won the most battles." Wanting to prepare for the time when she would be Heath's wife, Nancy read all of the newspapers and magazines that came into the Foster home, and the predominant news was about the war. "The Union lost two battles at Bull Run. And when they tried to conquer Richmond along the Virginia peninsula, they had to retreat."

"I'll admit," Heath said, "that the losses are embarrassing, but the Union seems to have trouble finding the right leadership. Now that Robert E. Lee is in command of the Army of Northern Virginia, it won't get any easier."

"If we could have had Stonewall Jackson on our side, it might have helped. He was a native of the western counties, so I don't know why he had to fight with the Confederacy."

Always willing to discuss political matters with Nancy, Heath delayed talking about the new house plans.

"The Union Army has made a poor showing in the attempt to take Richmond, but we need to look to the West. We've made great gains in the Mississippi River area."

Indicating places he had marked on the map, Heath said, "Union victories at Fort Henry and Fort Donelson gave the nation a new hero in Ulysses S. Grant. A subsequent Union victory at Shiloh and the capture of New Orleans gave us control of the Mississippi River and cut the Confederacy in two."

"But the Confederates are still in Vicksburg."

Heath laughed and playfully chucked her under the chin. "Why are you so pessimistic tonight — throwing cold water on all of my ideas? The Southerners are tough, but they can't compete with the military and industrial might of the North. Our navy has thrown a blockade around the South. They can't ship their cotton. They can't get any armaments, medical supplies, or food through the blockade. England and France haven't recognized the Confederacy as a separate nation, and they aren't likely to."

"You're looking at the situation on a larger scale than I do."

He nodded. "Right from the first, the Union has waged an offensive war, and they're always harder to win. As a physician, I deplore the loss of human life, and the longer the war drags on, the more men are going to be killed. I wish I could change that, but I can't."

He took her hand and drew her forefinger along the crooked chain of mountains dividing the proposed state of West Virginia from the eastern seaboard. "If all else fails, these mountains will stand strong. They provide a good barrier between us and an invasion by enemy forces. We can wage a war on this side of the mountains and still keep our state free."

Nancy looked at him with wondering eyes. "*We* could wage a war? Do you mean you would fight if it comes to that?"

"I hope I'm never forced to, but I've always said that I would defend my home and my loved ones against the enemy. Does that answer satisfy you, my little one?"

She stood on tiptoes and kissed him. "I won't say again that I think we'll lose the war."

"Good! And don't think it, either," he said as he gathered her into his arms and returned her kiss. "Let's make plans for our dream house."

"When I forget about the war, I get excited about our wedding. But I hate to leave Pa alone."

"I don't figure your father will be alone very long. He's not an old man, and he's a good catch. He'll probably take a wife."

Nancy's eyes widened. "I've wondered for years why he never remarried, and I finally figured he never would, whatever the reason."

"Would it bother you?"

"I don't think so. Mama has been gone a long time, and I wouldn't want him growing old alone."

"Do you have any ideas about our house?"

"I like that little brown house on Byron Street."

"You mean where the Baxters live?"

She nodded.

"It's small."

"But at first, I wouldn't want a big house." She waved her hand to indicate his present home. "A house this size would be too big for me to take care of by myself, and I'd still want to help your mother with this one. Wouldn't it be better to build a home with four or five rooms and add more rooms when we have a family?" She blushed and looked away from him.

He lifted her chin, and she met his eyes.

"Then you do want to have children."

"Of course — that's just the way it happens. You get married and you have babies."

"But some women don't particularly want a family. I'm glad to know that you do."

Conscious of the fact that in a few months she would leave her father's home, Nancy took three trips on the *Wetzel* with him during the months of February and March. Those journeys drew Nancy even closer to her father, but she was looking forward to her marriage. When she was with Heath, they made plans for their coming wedding and new home. With a few modifications, Heath had an architect draw plans for the kind of house Nancy wanted. Their dwelling was under construction by April 20 when President Lincoln announced that the act passed by Congress to admit West Virginia into the Union as the thirty-fifth state would take effect in sixty days.

"Will our house be finished by then?" Nancy asked.

"It should be. Why?"

"Let's get married the same day, on June 20."

Heath picked her up and swung her around the room.

"That sounds wonderful to me. We can

always celebrate two great occasions on the same day."

When she left the Foster house the next afternoon, Nancy detoured to go by the Danford home. Stella ran to let her in. "It's so good to see you. It's been a raw day outside, and I haven't gone out. Mama is in the kitchen."

As she walked with Stella down the hallway, Nancy remembered how beautiful this house had been before the war, and it saddened her to think of all the heirloom furniture that had been destroyed. "Mama is making a pie out of canned blackberries," Stella whispered, her eyes sparkling.

To everyone's amazement, Mrs. Danford, who had always been a lady of leisure supposedly suffering from ill health, had become a completely different woman in the aftermath of the family's financial losses. With Stella's help, Mrs. Danford had taken over the cleaning and operation of the household. And to her own surprise, she enjoyed cooking, and in no time, she was turning out excellent meals. Her contributions to church fellowship dinners were as popular as food prepared by longtime cooks. And there wasn't a healthier woman in all of Wheeling.

The luscious smell of baking pastry wafted

down the hallway, and Nancy smiled at Stella. Mrs. Danford was just lifting the pie from the oven as the girls entered the room. Thickened berry juice oozed from vent holes in the flaky crust.

"That's a masterpiece," Nancy said. "I'm sure it tastes as good as it smells and looks."

Mrs. Danford hugged Nancy. "Sit down and tell us the news while the pie cools, and I'll let you sample it."

"You look mighty happy," Stella commented.

"I am. Heath and I have set June 20 as the date for our wedding."

"That's less than two months away," Mrs. Danford said.

"Stella, will you stand up with me?"

Stella squealed and hugged Nancy.

"Yes, yes," she said. "I'm so happy for you."

"Are you going to have a big wedding?" Mrs. Danford asked.

"No. With the war still going on and everybody so hard up, we intend to keep everything simple. But we are going to be married at the church and invite any of our friends who want to come. Pa is going to stand up with us, too."

"Isn't that the date Papa said West Virginia will become a state?"

Nancy nodded happily. "That's the reason we chose that day."

As she moved around putting pieces of steaming pie in bowls, Mrs. Danford said, "You should have a new dress anyway. I'd like to make it for you."

"Now that Mama has learned to sew, she always wants to make new clothes."

"That would be wonderful," Nancy said.

"Perhaps Mrs. Foster will want to make your dress," Mrs. Danford said with some disappointment.

"I'll ask her, but she's so busy with the soldiers' canteens and knitting items for the needy that she wouldn't have enough time."

"We'll go shopping next week to see if there are any dry goods in Wheeling. If not, we can rip up some of our dresses and make it. I had a ball gown in the long ago, and I have no use for it anymore," she added without resentment. "We might use that."

Stella's mother had come a long way, Nancy thought and looked fondly at the woman who had lost so much in wealth and position, but had gained much more in things that really mattered.

With the completion of their home, the making of the wedding dress, and Nancy's involvement in the war effort, the two months passed more rapidly than she could have believed. During the last week that she would spend in her home on the banks of the Ohio, Nancy walked from one room to the other, touching the items that had always been a part of her life. How would it seem to move into a home where she couldn't even see the river?

Perhaps sensing that she was having difficulty coping with the changes marriage would bring, two days before the wedding, Heath suggested that they take a picnic lunch and spend the day by themselves.

Taking a deep breath as they drove away from the house toward the bridge that would take them into the state of Ohio, Nancy said, "Oh, it is good to be alone with you. I want our wedding day to be wonderful — something we can look back on the rest of our lives. And everything seems to be going wrong."

"What's troubling thee, sweet?" Heath asked. "I brought thee away from town to set thy mind at ease. But we might as well talk about whatever is troubling thee so we can put it behind us. Go ahead and tell me."

"The current talk is that Confederate forces are going to invade Wheeling to stop the inauguration of Governor Boreman. They've captured two towns in the eastern panhandle, and the commanders of state militia have been alerted to mobilize their troops."

"We're a long way from those towns."

When Heath turned to access the bridge that led to the state of Ohio, they saw that a barrier had been placed across the bridge, and two armed militiamen held up a hand to stop them.

"Whoa!" Heath said, muttering under his breath, "What's going on?"

Nancy clutched his arm.

The man who approached the buggy must have recognized Heath, for he said, "Where're you going, Doc? Somebody sick?"

"No. Nancy and I are going for a drive."

"We can't let you cross into Ohio. You'll have to do your drivin' somewhere else. You don't have a reputation of bein' favorable to the Union cause anyway."

Nancy had seldom seen Heath display anger, but he raked the man with a withering stare. He opened his mouth to speak but apparently changed his mind. He backed the horse a short distance until he could turn around and start eastward.

"I don't understand," Nancy said. "Why won't they let us go into Ohio?"

"I don't know," he said in a choked voice.

"Dost thou have any idea where we can go now?"

"Let's walk down the river from our home to where there's a hickory nut grove with plenty of shade. We pick up a year's supply of nuts there every fall. There's a pretty view of the river."

In silence, they drove back to Nancy's home, and Heath tied his horse in the shade. Pa was working on steamboat equipment in his shop, and he looked surprised when they stopped in the doorway.

"Short picnic," he said.

"No picnic at all. The bridge into Ohio is blockaded — we weren't allowed to cross," Heath said.

Pa whistled and wiped his greasy hands on a rag. "Rumors have spread around that that was going to happen."

"Why?" Nancy asked.

"Two days ago, President Lincoln called for one hundred thousand troops from Pennsylvania, Maryland, Ohio, and West Virginia. Our state's quota was ten thousand." With an ironic grin, her father continued, "Wheeling folks who were awful patriotic two years ago have seen what war's like, and they want no part of it. Seems like a lot of local men tried to leave town yesterday to avoid the draft. The officials aim to stop them, or they won't get enough soldiers to fill the quota."

"That does seem like a lot of men from our few counties," Nancy said.

"There's more to it than that," Pa said. "The Army of Northern Virginia is as strong as it's ever been. After that big Confederate victory at Chancellorsville, General Lee is headin' north with his army. They might intend to take the federal capital, but the general feeling is that Lee plans to raid one of Pennsylvania's munitions factories. The Army of the Potomac is staying between the Confederates and Washington, so Lee is angling westward. It won't surprise me if there ain't a big fight in Maryland or Pennsylvania. The war is comin' closer to home now!"

"Yes, and that's why local residents aren't as enthusiastic about fighting as they were two years ago," Heath said.

"They ain't so worried that they've stopped gettin' ready for the big shindig they're throwin' two days from now. I was uptown yesterday and saw the large platform they're buildin' in front of Linsly Institute."

"That building will be the first statehouse. The program will be held there at eleven o'clock after the fourth and fifth regiments of the West Virginia militia march from the

McClure House to the institute."

"After your weddin' at nine o'clock," Pa mentioned.

"Yes," Nancy answered. "Mrs. Foster is serving wedding cake and coffee at her home afterward, but that will still give us time to attend the inaugural ceremonies."

"We'll go to the hickory nut grove for our picnic," Heath said, "if it's all right to leave my horse and buggy here."

"I'll keep an eye on 'em. You won't have any trouble with soldiers down on the point, but the locusts might pester you. I've never seen such swarms as we're havin' this year."

"I like to hear them sing," Nancy said.

"I don't call it singin'," Pa complained. "Just a humdrum buzz that gets on my nerves. Besides, they eat up too many leaves and gardens."

"All right," Nancy said, laughing. "I won't listen to them."

"You can't help it," Pa said, but he grinned. "Go on and enjoy yourselves."

Heath picked up the basket his mother had packed. The locusts' incessant humming did accompany them as they walked, but the sound of songbirds and the quacking of ducks on the river overpowered the locusts when they reached the shaded grove and spread out the food on a tablecloth.

"Even the president's call for more troops hasn't stopped the excitement of the launching of our new state," Heath said. "According to the paper, the hotels are already filled with visitors and dignitaries. The *Intelligencer* is full of ads. The stores think they can sell a lot of merchandise to make up for the loss they've taken during the hard times of the past six months."

The peace of the area tended to quell many of Nancy's concerns about the war, their coming wedding, and the change in her life. "Two days from now, we'll be married," she said with a tinge of sadness in her voice.

Heath reached for her hand. "Surely thou aren't having second thoughts!"

"No, but I've always dreaded change. I love you, and I want to marry you, spend the rest of my life with you — but there's a little sadness, too, that the first twenty years of my life have ended. I suppose everyone feels that way."

He kissed the fingers he held. "I'm su~ that all brides do, but it's been that v since the days of Adam and Eve when (told His first creation, 'Therefore sʰ man leave his father and his mothᵉ shall cleave unto his wife: and they one flesh.' God will bless our u~

sure of it." Attempting to direct her attention away from the past, he asked, "And how's the wedding dress coming along?"

"It's beautiful," she said happily "I can't believe that Mrs. Danford could take two of her old dresses and come up with such a beautiful gown. It's made out of cream taffeta trimmed with flat pleating, deep fringe, and large ribbon bows. And she fashioned a short veil out of a lace curtain." She didn't mention the ruffled pantalets and embroidered chemise that his mother had helped her to make.

"I hope I won't be too plain for thee," he said, his eyes twinkling. "I'm wearing my best black suit, which is only a year old, but Mother is making a new shirt for me."

"I know you'll look as handsome as always," she said. Moving close to him, she touched her lips to his. "I'm going to like being your wife."

Nancy sat wide-eyed beside the open window, breathing in the dank smell of the river and the droning of night insects, wondering if she would sleep at all. In spite of the anticipation of tomorrow, when she would marry Heath and when West Virginia would officially be admitted into the Union, she knew that the political situation of the nation would have its effect on the happiness they should enjoy as newlyweds.

The future of the new state was uncertain, for it was generally believed that Virginia would not willingly give up its western counties. And with Lee's army on the march, it was difficult to predict the future. She knelt beside her bed for a long time, asking God's blessing on her marriage to Heath, as well as His mercy on the nation.

Although she had only a few hours of sleep, Nancy got up at the usual hour, and when Pa came from his bedroom, she had a breakfast of oatmeal and eggs ready for him.

"You didn't have to cook for me this morning," he protested.

Her father was not a demonstrative man, and when he came to Nancy and put his arms around her, she started crying.

"Now! Now!" he said, patting her head, which she'd pressed against his chest. "I didn't mean to make you cry. But I want you to know how proud I am of you and thank you for bein' such a dutiful daughter. You've picked a good man, and I can't ask for nuthin' more than that you'll be the kind of wife to him that your ma was to me." He held her at arm's length and kissed her cheek. She noticed moisture in her father's eyes that she hadn't seen except at the funerals of her mother and brother. But he grinned through his tears, saying, "Now git busy and put my breakfast on the table. We don't want to keep your man waitin'."

Seventeen

Nancy had left her wedding clothes at the Danford house, and at her father's insistence, she let him wash the breakfast dishes while she hurried to their house.

Mrs. Danford greeted her at the door. "I've already filled the tub with water. And I bought a bar of fancy soap yesterday," she said. Nancy followed her into the kitchen. "You don't have to hurry. Mr. Danford went to the factory for a short time, and Stella and I won't disturb you. There's a fresh towel on the rack."

As Nancy reveled in the warm water, sniffing the violet-scented soap, she missed not having her own mother with her on her wedding day. "But I shouldn't complain," she said to herself. "Both Mrs. Foster and Stella's mother have been so good to me that I really won't miss a mother's love today."

Heath's mother had made her dainty linen

nightgowns. And they had nice furniture for their home. Heath had bought new oak furniture for their parlor, and Mrs. Foster had insisted that he take his bedroom suite from her house. She had also divided some of the crystal and china that had been in the Foster family for several years. Nancy had been particularly pleased with the gift of a Boston rocker that she'd used often during her hours in the Foster home.

"Are you about finished?" Stella called. "It'll take awhile to get into our new dresses."

Nancy stepped out of the tub and dried quickly. She didn't want to be late for her own wedding.

Shortly before nine o'clock, Nancy and Stella walked downstairs to join the Danfords for the short walk to the church. Mr. and Mrs. Danford wore two-year-old clothing like everyone else in Wheeling, but they appeared as elegant as they had looked when they were wealthy as they followed Nancy and Stella down the street to St. Matthew's Church.

Nancy had been pleased with her appearance after she'd surveyed herself in the floor-length mirror in Stella's bedroom. And she was even more gratified when people they met on the street paused to stare at her.

"We're getting a lot of attention," Stella whispered, and her brown eyes glistened with merriment. "It won't be long now," she added as they walked into the church.

Mr. Danford escorted the girls to the front pew where Heath and Pa sat. Nancy picked up the bouquet of white roses that Mrs. Foster had prepared for her. An unseen organist started playing softly, and the minister entered the sanctuary from a small door to the left. He shook hands with the members of the wedding party and motioned for them to stand. He asked Heath and Nancy to join hands.

Starting with God's creation of man and woman in Genesis, the pastor discussed the importance that God had placed on marriage. He mentioned some of the more memorable wedded couples in the Bible — Ruth and Boaz, Hannah and Elkanah, John and Elizabeth, Joseph and Mary. He closed the biblical meditation with a quotation from the book of Ephesians: "Let every one of you in particular so love his wife even as himself; and the wife see that she reverence her husband."

After they took their vows, Heath slipped a simple gold band on Nancy's ring finger.

The minister closed his Bible and concluded the service. "It has been my privilege to preside at this ceremony uniting Heath Foster and Nancy Logan in the bonds of sacred matrimony. What God has joined together, let no man put asunder." Smiling benignly, he added, "You may kiss your bride, Heath."

With hands that trembled slightly, Heath lifted Nancy's veil, and their kiss sealed for eternity the vow they had taken.

Stella's parents, Mrs. Foster, and several of their friends, including Tabitha Clark, quickly gathered around the wedding party to congratulate them. "All of you are invited to a wedding breakfast at our home," Mrs. Foster said, "which we can enjoy and still have time to get in place before the inauguration ceremony starts."

During the short walk to the Foster home, Heath held Nancy's hand. "It's a proud day for me, but also one that has humbled me. I don't have the words to tell thee how much it means to me that thou actually want to be my wife. While the preacher talked, I made my own private vow, promising God that I would never let thee be sorry you married me."

Clouds had gathered by the time they

finished their breakfast, and Heath must have noticed that Nancy was worried about getting her wedding dress wet. Before they left the house, he picked up a large umbrella from the hall tree. "This will keep us dry," he promised. The sun peeked in and out of the clouds as the wedding party hurried to the roof of a store building near Linsly Institute to watch the festivities, but Nancy was trusting that it wouldn't rain.

The new state officials sat on the platform in front of the institute. Eager spectators crowded every rooftop, nearby streets, and private yards. When Reverend J. T. McClure stepped to the podium and removed his hat, a sudden hush fell over the noisy crowd.

Nancy's own heart and mind echoed the words of the minister as he prayed, "Almighty God, we pray that this state, born amidst tears and blood and fire and desolation, may long be preserved, and from its little beginning may grow to be a power that shall make those who come after us look upon it with joy and gladness and pride of heart."

When Governor Pierpont, who had so skillfully and patiently guided the Reorganized Government of Virginia, gave his farewell speech, he said, "My desire is to see West Virginia free from all shackles. I pray that she may from this small beginning grow to be the proudest member of the glorious galaxy of states that form the nation."

The crowd cheered when Arthur I. Boreman stood to take the oath of office as the new governor. Nancy looked at him with interest. It was rumored that the new governor was an unyielding man, but Heath had said that was a necessary attribute for any man taking over the reins of a new state with such a stormy background. A man in his late thirties, Boreman had a stern face dominated by a long black beard, and Nancy was impressed by his appearance and his acceptance speech. She especially liked his pledge to establish a system of education that would give every child, whether rich or poor, an education to fit them for responsible positions in society.

After the speechmaking ended, men removed their hats and the crowd stood at attention. Thirty-five girls representing each state in the Union sang the "Star-Spangled Banner," accompanied by the band. Overcome by pride in her state, as well as the nation, Nancy wiped her eyes with a lace handkerchief.

A captain of the militia stepped forward.

"Let's hear three cheers for the state of West Virginia," he called.

The cheers were deafening, and Nancy wished they were loud enough to be heard all the way to Richmond.

"Now three more cheers for the United States of America."

Again the sounds of rejoicing echoed from the bluffs east of Wheeling and across the river to the hills of Ohio. When the ceremony ended, Heath and Nancy mingled with the crowds milling around the streets of the city, waiting for evening to come when they could watch the fireworks display. Although they had seen a lot of Tabitha Clark in the past year, to Nancy's knowledge, her father had never taken any notice of her, but when Tabitha took hold of Pa's arm and they wandered off together, Nancy quickly exchanged a surprised glance with her new husband. Heath grinned at her and lowered his left eyelid in a significant wink.

By six o'clock, Nancy thought she couldn't walk another step, and it was still four hours before the fireworks started. Perhaps noting her fatigue, Heath said, "Let's go home, Nancy. We can have supper, rest awhile, and come out again for the closing celebration."

"Yes," she said. "My wedding clothes are

hot, and I'd like to change into something cooler."

Their family and friends had been lost in the crowd, and they turned toward their new home alone. Nancy went into the bedroom and changed her wedding gown for a white linen dress she had brought to the house the day before. While they discussed the events of the day, she served the supper that Mrs. Foster had prepared. Mealtime had been a silent time in the Logan home, but Nancy and Heath discussed the day's festivities, as was the custom of the Foster family.

When it started to get dark, Heath said, "It's time to go now."

Nancy sat on the sofa and bit her lip. When she didn't answer, Heath persisted, "Or dost thou not want to see the fireworks?"

"Not really. Do you?"

He replied by pulling her up into his arms, and Nancy surrendered to his embrace. She was shy about the intimacies of marriage awaiting her, but she loved Heath and looked forward to whatever the future held for them.

EPILOGUE

April 1865

Nancy had just finished nursing her two-month-old son when she heard the back door open. She didn't want to waken Clayton, so she continued rocking slowly in the Boston rocker.

"I'm home," Heath called as he always did when he returned from a call.

"I'm in the parlor," she said quietly.

He bent to kiss Nancy and touched Clayton's tiny fingers curled on his mother's breast.

"I love thee," he whispered. "Both of you."

She smiled at him. "If you'll take the baby and put him in his cradle, I'll finish supper."

He laid the newspaper he carried on the table beside her and took Clayton from her arms. Wondering at his significant look, she picked up the paper and read the prominent headline: LEE SURRENDERS TO GRANT AT

APPOMATTOX.

"It's finally over," Heath said.

Nancy didn't know whether to shout with joy that the war had ended at last or weep in remorse over the tragic events that had torn the country apart. As she worked at the stove, finishing preparation of the food, she reflected on the things that had happened since they had been married.

Not long after their wedding, two events had struck the death knell of the Confederacy. After months of siege, Vicksburg had finally surrendered, which paved the way for the Union's complete control of the Mississippi River. And on that same day, July 4, 1863, the Confederate Army started the slow trip back to Virginia after being defeated at Gettysburg, Pennsylvania. Even then, the Confederacy held on, and the months since then had cost the lives of thousands of young men. Knowing how she had mourned her brother's death, Nancy's heart was burdened daily for families who were experiencing the same sorrow that she and Pa still felt.

Grateful for the good news, Nancy whispered, "Thank You, God, that the war has finally ended. Have mercy on us as a nation and heal our wounds."

Coming into the kitchen, Heath said,

"Theoretically, we're one nation again."

"And I thank God for that," she said, "but how long will it take to heal the wounds inflicted by four years of warfare?"

As he sat at the table, Heath said, "Longer than it took to fight the war. There's too much ill will and hatred on both sides now. I tremble for what the future holds. Our people have lost the innocence they had at the beginning of the war."

"I'm certainly not the girl I was when the war started."

"I know," he said with a grin as he served her a helping of beef stew. Switching from *thee* to *you* in his conversation as he often did, Heath continued, "Instead of the sassy girl who stood up to Tabitha Clark, you have become a devoted wife, mother — an attractive matron who's up on all the current news and can discuss the classics as if you grew up reading them. You're quite a challenge for me to live up to."

"Disappointed?" she asked.

Suddenly serious, he said, "Not at all. Thou art all I could ever have dreamed for in a wife. You have made me very happy."

She blew a kiss across the table. "Now that other doctors will be returning from the war, maybe you can proceed with the medical research you came to Wheeling to do."

"I intend to." As he helped himself to another serving of stew, he speculated, "I thought that was my reason for coming west, but now I know that God sent me here to meet you. I never forget to thank Him for that."

"Tabitha stopped by today," Nancy said, "to bring a blanket she made for Clayton. After turning out to help your mother and the rest of us make items for the soldiers — Union soldiers, mind you — she's become a good knitter. She said Pa's taking the *Wetzel* out in the morning." Reminiscently, she added, "I think that of all the surprises I've had over these years, the most amazing was when Pa and Tabitha got married."

"That didn't surprise me," Heath said. "I told you Wendell wouldn't stay single long after you left home." He slanted a teasing look at Nancy. "I'm still curious why their marriage didn't bother thee."

Giving him a minxlike smile, she said, "After having such a happy marriage with you, I think everyone should enjoy wedded bliss. Besides, I forgave Tabitha long ago for the way she treated me. If she hadn't been so mean, you probably never would have noticed me. I couldn't be mad at her when she's made Pa happy. And it does my heart good to see the way he dotes on Tommy."

"The way Tommy has taken to life on the river may have saved the boy's life. He's much stronger since he's been traveling on the boat with Wendell."

She walked to the oak sideboard and brought the Bible to him for their nightly reading. "I'm thankful that God has brought an end to the war and that Wheeling wasn't overrun by the enemy. Can you think of something to read that will sum up the last four years?"

"I know exactly what I want to read. For weeks when it was obvious that the war would end soon, I've thought many times about the incident when His disciples asked Jesus to give a sign of His second coming. He said, " 'And when ye shall hear of wars and rumours of wars, be ye not troubled: for such things must needs be; but the end shall not be yet.' "

Turning to the Old Testament, Heath said, "God hates conflict, but I suppose we will have wars until Jesus returns to earth for His followers. But I always take comfort in the words of Isaiah when he talked about the latter days.

" 'And he shall judge among the nations, and shall rebuke many people: and they shall beat their swords into plowshares, and their spears into pruning hooks: nation shall

241

not lift up sword against nation, neither shall they learn war any more.' I believe that Isaiah was prophesying about the second coming of Jesus. So no matter how many wars come our way, we have that to look forward to."

"I pray that our country will never be divided again and that all wars will cease."

"Amen, darling! That's my wish, too. But I don't foresee that happening in our lifetime." He laid the Bible on the table, stood, and pulled Nancy into a tight embrace. "But as long as we face the future together, I'll be content, for I love thee."

Snuggling close to him, Nancy gave herself freely to the promise of his kiss.

ABOUT THE AUTHOR

Irene B. Brand published her first books in 1984. She became a Barbour author in 1990. By the end of 2007, she will have had forty-four books published with another one contracted for 2008. Irene lives with her husband, Rod, in Southside, West Virginia. She is active in her local Baptist church, where she teaches Sunday school, plays the piano and/or organ, directs the musical program, and serves as the treasurer.

The employees of Thorndike Press hope you have enjoyed this Large Print book. All our Thorndike, Wheeler, and Kennebec Large Print titles are designed for easy reading, and all our books are made to last. Other Thorndike Press Large Print books are available at your library, through selected bookstores, or directly from us.

For information about titles, please call:
  (800) 223-1244

or visit our Web site at:
  http://gale.cengage.com/thorndike

To share your comments, please write:
  Publisher
  Thorndike Press
  295 Kennedy Memorial Drive
  Waterville, ME 04901